HARLEQUIN®

Makes any time special ®

AVAILABLE THIS MONTH:

#913 THE IMPROPERLY PREGNANT PRINCESS
Jacqueline Diamond

#914 THE PLAYBOY'S OFFICE ROMANCE
Karen Toller Whittenburg

#915 WITH COURAGE AND COMMITMENT
Charlotte Maclay

#916 A QUESTION OF LOVE
Elizabeth Sinclair

HARLEQUIN®

915
March

AMERICAN *Romance*®

WITH COURAGE AND COMMITMENT

Charlotte Maclay

ENGI
LADD

MEN
of
Station
Six

5

Stephanie looked up and her heart did a ridiculous stutter step.

Danny Sullivan stood there in his navy blue dress uniform, the pants and shirt perfectly creased as though he were about to stand inspection, his badge glistening. His midnight-black hair was combed back, the usually unruly curls tamed for the moment. She had an almost irrepressible urge to muss his hair with her fingers, to—

She didn't want to go there. Not now. Not in the presence of twenty wide-eyed preschoolers.

Nor did she want to admit how her lungs seized when his eyes snared her, their color almost as bright as the royal blue the children used to color the sky in their paintings.

But he'd made it pretty obvious he didn't like kids. They made him nervous. Very soon she'd be having a baby, who would quickly turn into a kid. Bottom line—Danny Sullivan wouldn't be interested in pursuing a personal relationship with her.

Not in this lifetime....

Dear Reader,

March roars in like a lion this month with Harlequin American Romance's four guaranteed-to-please reads.

We start with a bang by introducing you to a new in-line continuity series, THE CARRADIGNES: AMERICAN ROYALTY. The search for a royal heir leads to some scandalous surprises for three princesses, beginning with *The Improperly Pregnant Princess* by Jacqueline Diamond. CeCe Carradigne is set to become queen of a wealthy European country, until she winds up pregnant by her uncommonly handsome business rival. Talk about a shotgun wedding of royal proportions! Watch for more royals next month.

Karen Toller Whittenburgh's series, BILLION-DOLLAR BRADDOCKS, continues this month with *The Playboy's Office Romance* as middle brother Bryce Braddock meets his match in his feisty new employee. Also back this month is another installment of Charlotte Maclay's popular series, MEN OF STATION SIX. Things are heating up between a sexy firefighter and a very pregnant single lady from his past—don't miss the igniting passion in *With Courage and Commitment*. And rounding out the month is *A Question of Love* by Elizabeth Sinclair, a warm and wonderful reunion story.

Here's hoping you enjoy all that Harlequin American Romance has to offer you—this month, and all the months to come!

Best,

Melissa Jeglinski
Associate Senior Editor
Harlequin American Romance

WITH COURAGE AND COMMITMENT
Charlotte Maclay

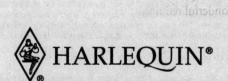

HARLEQUIN®

TORONTO • NEW YORK • LONDON
AMSTERDAM • PARIS • SYDNEY • HAMBURG
STOCKHOLM • ATHENS • TOKYO • MILAN • MADRID
PRAGUE • WARSAW • BUDAPEST • AUCKLAND

ISBN 0-373-16915-9

WITH COURAGE AND COMMITMENT

This edition published by arrangement with Harlequin Books S.A.

® and TM are trademarks of the publisher. Trademarks indicated with ® are registered in the United States Patent and Trademark Office, the Canadian Trade Marks Office and in other countries.

Visit us at www.eHarlequin.com

Printed in U.S.A.

ABOUT THE AUTHOR

Charlotte Maclay can't resist a happy ending. That's why she's had such fun writing more than twenty titles for Harlequin American Romance, Duets and Love & Laughter, as well as several Silhouette Romance books. Particularly well-known for her volunteer efforts in her hometown of Torrance, California, Charlotte's philosophy is that you should make a difference in your community. She and her husband have two married daughters and four grandchildren, whom they are occasionally allowed to baby-sit. She loves to hear from readers and can be reached at: P.O. Box 505, Torrance, CA 90508.

Books by Charlotte Maclay

HARLEQUIN AMERICAN ROMANCE

WHO'S WHO AT FIRESTATION SIX

Danny Sullivan—Wanted to follow in Chief Gray's footsteps, but he never imagined the chief's pesky daughter could teach him about love and family.

Stephanie Gray—The fire chief's daughter returns home six months pregnant and unmarried, and discovers the boy next door she once idolized has matured into the man she can love forever.

Harlan Gray—The dedicated fire chief will go to the wall for his men; the only thing he can't do is escape a pursuing councilwoman.

Councilwoman Evie Anderson—Has her eye on the most eligible widower in town, Chief Gray, and is gaining ground.

Emma Jean Witkowsky—The dispatcher has an uncanny way of predicting the future, especially when it comes to matters of the heart.

Tommy Tonka—An adolescent genius when it comes to mechanical things, but he needs help from his firefighter friends when it comes to girls.

Mack Buttons—The station mascot, a five-year-old chocolate Dalmatian who loves kids, people and the men of Station Six.

Chapter One

Siren wailing, Engine 62 roared out of the station house and turned onto the main street of Paseo del Real in central California.

Riding backward behind the driver, Danny Sullivan tightened his shoulder harness, aware of the pleasant hum of adrenaline flowing through his veins. This is what a firefighter lived for—a chance to use his training. To put a little wet on the red, to douse a fire with water or foam.

"This could be a bad one," his buddy Greg Wells in the adjacent seat commented. "Dispatch said it was a preschool."

"Yeah, I heard." Danny didn't relish the thought of kids trapped in a structure fire, scared, maybe even hysterical. Definitely hard to manage. Rescue would be the first order of business. "Let's hope they have sprinklers and that they worked."

Looking relaxed, Wells settled into his seat. "I was kinda hoping they'd have a couple of cute teachers."

Chuckling, Danny nodded his agreement. Between the two of them, he and Greg had an ongoing competition to see who got the first date with any good-looking single woman they happened to rescue from a fire. So far they were neck and neck. It was time for Danny to apply a little pressure, prove the Irish were head and shoulders above any Englishman—three generations removed or not—when it came to romance.

The engine peeled off the main drag of town onto a side street lined with small businesses and drab apartment houses, then pulled to a stop in front of a one-story structure with a fenced yard filled with kid's play equipment. Gray smoke drifted up from the back half of the building, a good omen suggesting things weren't totally out of hand. The brightly painted sign over the front entrance read Storytime Preschool.

With a flick of his wrist, Danny released his harness, grabbed his air pack and hopped down from the cab. He headed to the back of the truck for the hose.

"Thank goodness you're here!" a woman cried. "We have to get them out."

He turned, had a fleeting glimpse of short brown hair, a familiar face and the flash of a bright yellow blouse before she raced away toward the front door of the building.

"Stephanie?" When the heck had she come back to town?

He cursed and ran after her. Kids still had to be inside. Otherwise the fire chief's daughter would have more sense than to go running into a burning building. But then, growing up on the same block where she lived, Danny knew Stephanie Gray could be damn mulish when she made up her mind about something.

He took the porch steps in one leap and burst through the open door. "Stephanie! Where are you?" A fire alarm was still ringing off its mount but there wasn't much smoke, only the lingering acrid scent of burning wood and fabric. The sprinklers must have done their job. But no sign of kids, either, only building blocks and toy trucks hastily abandoned in the middle of the room.

"In here! Help me!"

He followed the sound of her voice toward the back of the house, his heart pumping.

"Oh, the poor little things," she cried. "Hurry."

God, he dreaded what he'd find. Injured kids were the worst. He could only hope he was in time to—

She thrust a small metal cage into his arms. "Take Arnold outside. I'll bring Polly. We'll have to try mouth-to-mouth resuscitation."

"We'll what?" Dumfounded, he stared at the cage. My God, she'd handed him a hamster, who was lying motionless on his side in a pile of wood shavings. "What about the kids?" He whirled, looking for an unconscious child curled up in a corner. Or a hot spot the sprinklers hadn't entirely cooled.

"They're fine." With her arms around a matching cage, she shoved him back toward the front of the house. "They're all outside at our assembly point."

"You're telling me—" She'd risked her neck— and his—for a couple of hamsters? Somehow, it figured.

Greg and Jay Tolliver from Engine 61 brushed past him, pulling a length of two-inch hose through the building as he went out the door. Their gazes rested on the cage he gripped in his hand.

"Great rescue, Sullivan," Greg said, grinning. "Way to go!"

So great, Danny was likely to get razzed about this for months. At least until somebody else at Station 6 did something equally *heroic.*

"Hurry up." Stephanie placed the cage she was carrying on the ground well away from the refurbished house, kneeling beside it. "The poor little things can't be without air long."

"You really expect me to give a hamster mouth-to—"

The expression she shot him practically made him bleed. If he didn't do this, he'd be toast in the department. Not that her old man would do anything overt, but Stephanie *was* the chief's daughter. Hell, Danny hadn't even known she was back in town. Last he'd heard she was in San Francisco. Just his luck she'd shown up here during his shift, in the middle of a fire, with a frazzled hamster needing kissy-face resuscitation.

With a muttered curse, Danny lifted *Arnold* out of the cage. Damn, he'd never live this one down.

POLLY GAVE A TINY COUGH, shuddered and began breathing on her own.

With a relieved sigh, Stephanie Gray settled back on her haunches. It was bad enough that the candle-making project had gone so desperately awry. She didn't know what she would have done if she'd had to explain to the children that their pet hamsters had died of smoke inhalation.

She glanced over at Danny to see how he was doing. All turned out in his bunker pants, heavy jacket and helmet, he looked bigger and taller and broader than she remembered him. But her recollections were quite clear of his flashing blue eyes—Irish eyes—and wickedly sexy smile. As an adolescent, she'd spent hours spying on him down the block, making up any excuse to stroll by when he was outside. Not that he'd noticed.

Unfortunately she had his attention now, and he was scowling.

"Didn't your dad teach you anything about fires? You could have been killed going back in there."

She gave him her sweetest, most innocent smile. "But you were there to save me, weren't you? Like always."

"Just because one time I pulled you out of a tree when you got stuck doesn't mean I'm going to save your bacon every time you get in trouble."

If only he could. But no one could help her out of the mess she'd gotten herself in this time, which is why she'd moved home, her tail figuratively between her legs.

"So how'd the fire start?" Idly he stroked Arnold, who appeared to be breathing again. Feeling pretty grumpy, too, because the damn hamster bit down on

Danny's thumb. He swore. Loudly. Stuffed Arnold back into his cage, and gave his hand a quick shake.

"Hush. You can't use those kind of words in front of the children."

Warily he eyed the preschoolers, who had lined up along the outside of the fence. Alice Tucker, Stephanie's friend and the owner of the preschool, had them well in hand.

"Are Arnold and Polly gonna be okay?" Bobby Richardson asked.

"They're fine, children," Stephanie answered.

"Unless I strangle the one with the fangs," Danny grumbled under his breath.

Stephanie swallowed a laugh. Despite his gruff, macho exterior, Danny was among the sweetest, most sympathetic guys she'd ever known. She'd seen him put baby birds back in their nest when they'd fallen out and stand up for younger children who were being bullied by bigger kids. Though she'd never tell him she knew the truth about him. It would ruin the tough image he'd tried to project ever since his father had deserted him and his mother. Danny had been about ten at the time.

The rest of the firefighters were coming back out of the building now, coiling the hoses to put them back on the truck.

"Thanks, gentlemen," she called to them with a wave.

"There's still a pretty big mess in the kitchen," the battalion chief told her. "We'll get it cleaned up for you. Won't we, Sullivan?" he said pointedly.

"Yes, sir." Danny got to his feet.

Awkwardly Stephanie did, too. She knew the instant Danny realized she was pregnant, six months along but on her otherwise slender frame it looked as though she were carrying an elephant.

His eyes widened and his jaw dropped halfway to his knees. "Stephanie? Twiggy? What the hell happened to you?"

She didn't know which irritated her more—the fact that he'd used his old nickname for her when she'd been a skinny thirteen-year-old or the sudden surge of shame that coursed through her.

Lifting her chin, she looked square into his piercing blue eyes. "Same thing that happens to a lot of women." She'd thought she was in love, accidentally got pregnant and found out the feeling wasn't reciprocated.

"Man, I didn't even know you were married."

She winced but she could hardly keep her marital status a secret when he still lived down the street from her father's house where she was staying. Temporarily. "I'm not."

If anything, he looked more stunned than when he'd realized she was pregnant. He opened his mouth to speak then slammed it shut again.

"Hey, Sullivan!" one of the men shouted. "You gonna talk all day to that pretty lady or are you gonna earn your salary for a change?"

He glanced over his shoulder then back to Stephanie. "I, uh, gotta go. I'll see you around, huh?"

"Sure. We're neighbors, after all."

"Yeah, right." Turning, he jogged up to the porch and inside the building.

Well, she sure as heck had ruined her reputation with the tough guy down the street, hadn't she? She could only imagine what he was thinking now. The skinny, Goodie Two Shoes daughter of the fire chief had shown her true colors. She wasn't any better than any other woman and no more able to hang on to a boyfriend now than she had been when she'd worn braces in high school and had knobby knees.

She sighed. Unrequited adolescent infatuation didn't get any less painful at the age of twenty-five.

Picking up the two cages, she carried them to the children waiting by the fence. "Careful now," she warned them. "Polly and Arnold are a little upset by all the excitement. No fingers in the cages, remember."

The youngsters gathered around, oohing and aahing, reassuring each other and their pets that everything was all right. That wasn't precisely true, at least not for Stephanie. But she was determined that someday—someday soon—things would be all right again. She'd build a new life here in Paseo del Real. She'd raise her baby and they'd both be just fine, thank you very much.

So what if Danny now thought she was a slut?

"You really shouldn't have gone back in there," Alice said, her voice soft-spoken so the children wouldn't become upset. "With you being pregnant and all, the firemen would have—"

"Firefighters don't generally risk their lives for a

couple of hamsters.'' Guiltily she realized she'd put Danny at risk—and her baby—even though she'd known the sprinkler system had already squelched the flames. There could have been other hidden dangers. She'd simply lost her head in the urgency of the moment, anxious to rescue the childrens' pets. If her father heard about this particular stunt of hers, she'd be in deep yogurt. Harlan Gray was very protective of his men.

Of her, too, she admitted. Particularly so since her pregnancy had shown and she'd had to admit the truth. There would be no wedding in her future. She'd practically had to tie her father down to prevent him from driving to San Francisco and throttling Edgar Bresse with his bare hands.

With a sweet smile and an angelic face, Alice waggled her brows suggestively. ''That guy who brought out Arnold was certainly a hunk. Maybe we ought to have fires more often, at least small ones.''

''No, thanks.'' Danny was the last man on earth she'd wanted to see her pregnant and unwed. From now on, she'd keep her distance. Even if it was only across the street and a few houses down the block.

By now parents had heard about the fire and were arriving to pick up their children. Alice talked with each mom or dad, assuring them the damage had been slight, limited to the kitchen area. After a good airing and a little elbow grease, they would be open for business tomorrow morning.

Stephanie guessed it would take a *lot* of elbow grease to get the kitchen back in working order again.

They would have to make some adjustments for snacks and lunchtime.

"Miss Stephanie?" Bobby Richardson looked up at her with sad brown eyes. "I'm sorry I spilled the candle stuff."

"It's all right, honey." Kneeling, she hugged the four-year-old. He'd been acting silly and knocked over the hot paraffin, which then caught fire. They'd all been lucky no one had been burned. "It was an accident."

"You're not mad at me?"

"Of course not. Accidents happen." Just as unintentional pregnancies happen if you get a little careless, like when you're taking an antibiotic and you're on the Pill. That combination changes everything. "But we've both learned a good lesson about being careful, haven't we?"

Solemnly he nodded.

She squeezed him more tightly, his slender young body molding against hers. Someday soon she'd have a little girl as sweet and cuddly as Bobby, proving that "accidents" could be a blessing.

BACK AT THE STATION, Danny stripped to his Skivvies and headed for the shower. Greg was already there singing one of his favorite country-western tunes. Nobody had told him his voice was good. Just the opposite, in fact. Not that their kidding had slowed him down much. Hell, he probably would have brought his guitar into the shower with him if he hadn't been so protective of his precious instrument. Would have worn his Stetson, too, for that matter.

Truth was, Greg probably could have had a career in show biz but chose firefighting instead. That and helping operate his family's nearby cattle ranch, located on the rolling hills between Paseo and the coast.

"So, did you ask that hot-looking teacher out?" Greg asked.

Danny bristled. He knew who Greg meant, and she wasn't *hot*, at least he'd never thought of her that way. She was—hell, he didn't know what to think now. How could Stephanie have gotten pregnant and not have a husband? She wasn't that kind of girl. "No."

"Then she's still available, huh? Maybe I'll just drop by the preschool tomorrow when I—"

Danny grabbed him by the arm and swung him around. Soap suds flew in the air, spattering the white tile wall and across the floor. "What's the matter with you, man? Are you blind? She's pregnant. Didn't you see that?"

"Hey, ease up. I only got a glimpse of her, okay? I didn't know she was married."

"Yeah, well…" He wasn't about to tell Wells that the chief's daughter was pregnant and not married. It was none of Greg's business. None of his either. "So she's off-limits, okay?"

"Fine by me. I'm not eager to be a daddy anytime soon, anyway."

"Me, neither." And he resented like hell the stab of regret he'd felt when he'd realized Stephanie was pregnant—and he hadn't been the one to get her that way.

He had no idea where that thought had come from. It wasn't as if he'd ever so much as dated her. She'd been too damn young. Eight years his junior. And by the time she'd grown up, he was moving in a lot faster crowd than she could have handled, and her old man was the big boss in the fire department, for God's sake.

Which hadn't stopped Danny from keeping his eye on her over the years. Noticing her sexy little behind as she strolled by. Checking out her breasts when she'd gone from twiggy to nicely rounded.

Yeah, he'd kept an eye on her. And his hands off. That was still a good idea.

"So," Greg said as he turned off the shower and wrapped a towel around his waist. "What's it like to kiss a hamster?"

Jay Tolliver chose that exact moment to come into the shower room. "Looked to me like ol' hot lips here was enjoying himself. Whaddaya think?"

Mike Gables sauntered in, buck-naked like the rest of them. "The singles scene must really be getting tough if a hamster is the best our buddy can do. Maybe we oughta fix him up with Emma Jean downstairs. At least she could read his palm while he worked on his technique."

Danny groaned and shut off the shower. Emma Jean Witkowsky was the department's dispatcher and self-appointed gypsy fortune-teller, whose predictions more times than not were a hundred and eighty degrees wrong. Dating her was not an option he wanted to consider.

And he sure as hell didn't want to think about the next week or so until his buddies forgot all about the hamster incident. His next few shifts were going to be the pits.

His days off weren't going to be too swift, either, knowing Stephanie was living down the block again. And was pregnant with some other guy's baby.

When he returned to his quarters on the third floor of the main fire station, he discovered someone had cut out a big cardboard star and propped it on his bed. Across it they'd written #1 Rodent Kisser.

He groaned again. This was going to be a very long shift.

THAT EVENING, AFTER HOURS of scrubbing soot-stained walls, Stephanie placed a bubbling dish of vegetable lasagna on the table in front of her father. As a trade-off for her room and board, she was keeping house for her dad. Which had the added benefit of preventing his lady friend, Councilwoman Evie Anderson—a widow and Paseo del Real's worst cook—from bringing him meals. Tonight, though, Stephanie was so tired she would personally be willing to give Evie's culinary efforts a try.

"I understand you had some excitement at the preschool today."

Her hands stilled on the salad bowl she was about to deliver to the table. Had the word gotten back to him about the Great Hamster Rescue?

"We had a small fire," she said casually. "Nothing too dramatic."

"Two engines and a rescue unit rolled on the call."

She set the salad down and took her seat across from her father. "Good response time, too. You can be pleased about that."

He nodded and dished some lasagna onto her plate then served himself. At age sixty-three, he was still as fit as he had been at thirty, Stephanie suspected, although his hair was gray now and he wore it in a short butch cut.

"Evidently Alice was happy," he commented.

Stephanie's brows shot up. "She called?" When? They'd both been scrubbing—

"Yep. Seems the kids were so impressed with my firefighters they want to give one of them an award. Danny Sullivan, as a matter of fact."

Fortunately Stephanie hadn't taken a bite of food yet because she would have choked. She forced a smile. "Really? How nice."

"That's right." He forked some lasagna into his mouth. "Seems he saved Arnold's life. Pretty courageous of him, I'd say."

She nodded, thinking it was time for her to get an apartment of her own—before her father threw her out for putting one of his men at risk.

"I've always liked Danny, even when he was a little wild as a kid. You know, he's our top man on the department's triathlon team."

"I guess I hadn't heard that." Although she did know fire departments across the country were always coming up with one athletic contest or another in order to encourage physical fitness.

"Yep. Without Danny, Paseo wouldn't have a chance of winning the state finals this spring."

"Interesting." All the more reason her father was about to hand her her head on a platter for making Danny rescue a hamster.

Harlan Gray glanced up from his meal and gave her a fatherly smile. "Why don't we do something nice for him, like invite him over for dinner some night?"

She gaped at her father as he resumed eating his meal with obvious relish. That was it? She wasn't going to get the lecture on fire prevention? Safety first? The importance of human life, which included his men?

A seriously uncomfortable feeling raised the hackles on the back of her neck. Her father couldn't be doing a little matchmaking, could he? In cahoots with her friend Alice? She knew her father was distressed about her not being married. But she was in no condition to be *matched* with anyone.

Besides, what man in his right mind would be interested in a woman whose silhouette would soon resemble a blimp?

When she finally took a bite of dinner, the taste was bitter, much like the knowledge that if Danny hadn't been interested in her years ago, he certainly wouldn't be now.

Chapter Two

"You shouldn't be doing that." Danny wheeled his racing bike up behind Stephanie's ancient Honda, which was parked in her driveway, the trunk open. He'd been about to go out for a training run on his day off when he'd spotted Stephanie hauling heavy sacks of groceries into the house.

She straightened with a sack in her arms. "Doing what?"

"Lifting heavy stuff. Pregnant women aren't supposed to do that."

"So now you're an expert on pregnant women?"

"Evidently I know more than you do."

"Being pregnant is not a physical disability. I'm fine."

More than fine. She had the usual fire in her eyes, golden embers and hot sparks shooting in his direction. She'd been an imp as a youngster. As a woman, she was—

On a sudden surge of irritation, he unsnapped his bike helmet, rolled his bike out of sight behind some bushes near the back door, then took the sack from her arms. "You go sit somewhere. I'll bring in the groceries."

"Oh, for pity sake! I'm not disabled."

"Sit," he ordered and marched inside, as familiar with the Gray's house as he was with his own. Not much had changed since he'd been here as an adolescent—Harlan Gray as close to a father as he'd had in those days, Mrs. Gray like a doting aunt. And Stephanie a pesky little sister.

Naturally Stephanie hadn't listened to him any more today than she had when she'd been younger. Instead she'd picked up another bag of groceries and followed him inside. She gave a little toss of her hair that set the waves bouncing and put the groceries on the counter. "There are two more bags in the car," she said with false sweetness. "If you really think poor little me can't handle it."

He glowered at her. "I'll get 'em."

"Oh, my, such a big, brave man," she crooned.

On the way past her, he almost gave her a friendly little swat on her backside as he might have when she was a kid. But she wasn't a kid anymore. She was a woman. A *pregnant* woman wearing a bright red oversize T-shirt with a yellow target in the middle. Suddenly he didn't know what to do with his hands except stick them into his pockets. Except his bicycle shorts didn't have pockets.

He grimaced as he walked back to the car to get the last of the groceries. He never should have stopped to help her. He'd known that. Perversely he hadn't been able to stop himself.

STEPHANIE SQUEEZED HER EYES shut and took a deep breath. If she'd thought Danny was overwhelmingly masculine in his bunker pants and turnout coat, she was blown away by him in a skintight riding shirt and thigh-hugging shorts. Every muscle from shoulder to calves was well defined. A classic sculpture created in the flesh. No doubt *warm* flesh.

None of which gave him the right to boss her around. She'd had enough of that with Edgar, both at the office and in their relationship. Served her right for getting involved with her employer. But he'd been so smooth, so sophisticated—

So uninterested in becoming a father until the twenty-second century.

"Where do you want this stuff?"

She whirled toward him. "Anywhere. I can handle it from here on my own." Because that's how she was going to be from now on—on her own with a baby to raise.

And no one to tell her what to wear to the opening night of the San Francisco opera or what she should prepare for a dinner party for seventeen of his closest friends, all of whom were big clients of his advertising agency, not friends at all.

"Great. I'll be on my way then. I've gotta workout for a big race."

"I know. A triathlon." She plucked a gallon of nonfat milk from the first sack and put it in the refrigerator. Danny lingered by the back door. Maybe if she got out the fly swatter—

"When did you get back in town?"

"About a week ago. Alice needed a part-time teacher. All things considered, it seemed like a good time to come home." There hadn't been any point in remaining in San Francisco longer. Edgar wasn't going to change his mind about the baby. After the way he'd acted these past few months, she didn't even want him to.

Danny's gaze slid to her belly. "So you're going to be staying a while in Paseo?"

She refused to flinch. "Indefinitely."

"That's great. Uh, I'm sure your dad's happy to have you home." He made a show of glancing around the room as though her pregnancy made him uncomfortable, which it probably did. "The place looks pretty much the same as when I was here last. I remember when your mom framed that painting."

Involuntary Stephanie glanced at the wall above the kitchen sink that displayed her blue-ribbon high school painting—a helter-skelter modern cubist affair of reds and blues with streaks of virtually every color to be found in a box of crayons. It was awful.

"Mom thought I was going to be the next Rembrandt."

"You got a scholarship. How wrong could she have been?"

In spite of herself, Stephanie smiled. It had been nice to have parents who believed in her, and she still missed her mother, who had died four years ago during Stephanie's senior year in college. "Commercial art was the best I could do."

He leaned against the doorjamb as though he had

nowhere else to go. "I'm pretty good with stick figures if you need some help with any of your projects."

She laughed. She couldn't help herself. "The only art I'm doing these days is the four-year-old variety. Mostly finger painting and setting candle wax on fire."

"Yeah, well, they tell me primitive styles are back in vogue."

She lifted her brows. "What do you know about primitive art styles?"

"Hey, I watch a lot of PBS when I'm riding my stationary bike, okay? Broadens the mind." He touched a two-finger salute to his forehead. "Unless you need some other heroic deed done, I gotta go. You know what they say about practice, practice, practice."

She swallowed another smile. The last time she'd heard that remark she'd been sixteen years old and it had been a comment about sexual prowess. She hadn't gotten the meaning then. She tried not to now, though the heat of a blush crept up her cheeks, and she became defensive. "I think I'll be able to manage without you—barely. You might want to leave a couple of quarts of blood and your cell phone number just in case some grand catastrophe happens and you're not here to rescue me."

"I recommend you call 911."

Now, that conjured an interesting image. Frustrated pregnant woman puts in an emergency call to the fire department to quench her hormonal upsurge—Daniel Sullivan specifically requested to fill the bill.

She couldn't even begin to imagine what Chief Gray would do about that kind of call coming into dispatch. Although Emma Jean at the station would probably be able to handle it with considerable aplomb, her silver gypsy bracelets jingling as she did.

Sighing, Stephanie wondered what Emma Jean would see in her crystal ball about her future. Right now the best Stephanie could see was that the chocolate ice cream she'd purchased—purely for medicinal reasons, of course—was melting. She reminded herself to worry about only one thing at a time.

Instinctively she slid her hand across her belly. The future would take care of itself whether she wanted it to or not.

STEPHANIE POURED SMALL amounts of blue paint into four paper cups, setting them on the miniature easels in preparation for the children's arrival at school.

"I don't see why you had to make such a big deal out of Danny Sullivan rescuing the hamsters," she complained to Alice, who was unstacking pint-size chairs from the play table. "It's not like he did anything all that brave."

"The children think he's a hero. And you do have to give him some credit for kissing a hamster."

"He did mouth-to—"

"Besides, I was talking to one of the other fireman after all the excitement was over. Turns out he's single, and the way he was looking at you I got the distinct impression—''

''Aha! You are trying to do some matchmaking. For your information, Danny and I go back a long way and there hasn't been a single ounce of chemistry between us.'' Not on his part, at any rate. Her adolescent angsting didn't count.

The angelic smile on Alice's face didn't quite match the devilment in her gray eyes. Happily married women with devoted husbands and the standard two-point-seven healthy children were the bane of all single women. Constitutionally unable to pass up an opportunity to matchmake.

''Well, you do need a daddy for your baby and if you two have a past—''

''No past, not like you mean. No future, either.'' She dumped red powder into a clean cup and mixed in some water, stirring more vigorously than was wise. ''I'm probably the last woman on earth he'd want to get involved with, even if I wasn't pregnant. Which I am. So just cool it, okay?''

Alice's retort was cut off by the arrival of the first two children of the day. She lifted her shoulders in an unconcerned shrug, then hurried to greet the preschoolers.

Stephanie frowned at the spatters of red across the newspaper she'd been using to protect the table—and at the matching spots on her blouse. Fortunately she liked wearing bright colors. The print on this particular maternity blouse was of a flower garden in full bloom with the words, ''From little seeds grow the most beautiful things.''

She sighed. At least the paint was washable.

For the next hour, she supervised outdoor play, the February morning so mild the kids only needed a light sweater to keep them warm. Then she brought the youngsters inside for juice and show-and-tell. Jason Swift announced that he'd stuck an ant up his nose yesterday, and Tami Malone shared the news that when her daddy slept on top of her mommy, her mommy made funny noises, but it was all right because they loved each other.

Stephanie ruled out both topics from any further discussion.

She was about to send them off for free play with blocks and plastic dump trucks and the indoor playhouse, when the front door opened. She looked up and her heart did a ridiculous stutter step.

Danny Sullivan stood there in his navy-blue dress uniform, the pants and shirt perfectly creased as though he were about to stand inspection, his badge glistening. His midnight-black hair was combed back, the usually unruly curls tamed for the moment. She had an almost irrepressible urge to muss his hair with her fingers, to thread her hands through the fullness until he looked like—

She didn't want to go there. Not now. Not in the presence of twenty wide-eyed preschoolers.

Nor did she want to admit how her lungs seized when his eyes snared hers, their color almost as bright as the royal-blue the children used to color the sky in their paintings.

Only when he stepped farther into the room and young Tami cried out, "He's gots a doggy!" did Stephanie notice Danny had brought the station's mascot with him. Mack Buttons, a chocolate Dalmatian with brown spots and a sweet disposition, waggled his tail as the preschoolers gathered around him. Looking a little uncertain about so many children, Danny ordered the dog to sit.

"Careful, children," Alice warned, snaring the most fearless of the youngsters who had surged forward. "Remember you need to ask before you pet a strange dog."

"But he's so pretty!" Tami insisted.

"Yes, I know. And I'm sure Fireman Sullivan will let you all have a chance to pet him." She hustled the children to the rug, asking them to make a story-time circle. Stephanie helped out by corralling those who failed to respond to the initial request.

Danny stood uncertainly at the edge of the rug while all the commotion went on around him. His gaze followed Stephanie. The room seemed to light up with her in it, everything else paling by comparison. Which was saying something given the rainbow-painted walls and bright splashes of color around the room.

He noticed how easily she touched the children, a brush of her hand on a shoulder to steer a kid in the right direction, a caress of her fingertips on a rosy cheek to elicit a smile.

In contrast, he felt like a giant among Lilliputians.

"Why don't you sit in the rocking chair in the center of the circle?" Stephanie suggested.

"I think I'd rather stand." It was better than being surrounded by a mob of giggling three- and four-year-olds.

"Is something the matter?"

"I don't have much experience with kids. They, uh, make me nervous."

She looked offended. "They won't bite."

"The hamster did."

"I wish you'd told Alice when she called that you don't like children, then we could have—"

"I like kids well enough," he protested. "I just don't have many occasions to be around them."

"Think of this as your chance to get used to them, then."

She took his hand, startling him with the feel of her slender fingers wrapped around his. A jolt of electricity shot up his arm. Not just static electricity but something high voltage. Sexual. Potent. With it came images of hot sweaty bodies—his and Stephanie's—and rumpled sheets.

Before he could analyze what had happened, she led him to the chair. He sat because the shock had sent his heart into overdrive. He wasn't supposed to feel *any* sexual attraction to Stephanie. And if he did feel any, he was supposed to keep it under tight wraps.

No way did he want to get involved with Harlan Gray's daughter. The girl who had pestered him through half of his life. A woman who was pregnant with another man's baby.

Buttons sat on the floor beside him, looking at the children expectantly.

Danny made it a point not to look at Stephanie. He didn't want to know if she'd felt the attraction flowing between them, too.

"Before we give Fireman Sullivan his hero's medal," Alice said to the children, "would any of you like to ask him a question about being a firefighter?"

A half dozen hands shot up. Alice gave the nod to a pixie blonde. "Do you get to turn on the siren?"

"No, that's the engineer's job—the driver of the fire truck. I sit in back."

His answer seemed to disappoint the little girl. Maybe he should have lied. A part of him wanted to impress the youngster—and Stephanie, too. But since her dad was the fire chief, she'd probably had her fill of sirens.

A boy asked, "Do you get scared?"

"Sometimes. But firefighters are very well trained. You all know fires can be dangerous and—"

"When were you scared?"

His gaze slid around the room. He had the kids' attention. Stephanie's, too. He didn't want her to know that bravery didn't always come easily. That sometimes the most courageous man could turn into a coward.

"I spent a couple of summers fighting forest fires

in Idaho. I was a smoke jumper. Do you know what that means?''

When the kids shook their heads, he explained that he parachuted out of a plane near a fire that couldn't be reached in any other way. He didn't tell them of the terror of his last jump, the fear that still had the power to wake him up in a sweat from a dead sleep.

''That can be kind of scary,'' he concluded after the briefest of explanations.

The questions got a little easier after that. Did he rescue cats from trees? Not usually. Was his helmet heavy? Not really, and he was sorry he hadn't brought his along so they could try it on. Finally little blondie asked if they could pet the doggie yet.

A frequent school visitor, Buttons tolerated the petting with his usual patience, giving only a small yip when one of the kids stepped on his toe.

Then came the medal presentation.

Danny squirmed uncomfortably in the chair as the day's designated ''pet feeders'' brought out the hamsters to witness the big event. Giving mouth-to-mouth to a rodent wasn't Danny's idea of being heroic. And every shift since last week, he'd been razzed by his buddies one way or the other. He'd be happy for everyone to forget the incident.

Solemnly two children carrying a blue velvet pillow marched in from the back of the room. They halted like little soldiers in front of Danny, an aluminum foil star with a red, white and blue ribbon resting on the pillow. The little girl gave him a shy

smile. In a few years she'd be a killer, the boys unable
to resist her.

"Let's ask Miss Stephanie to put the medal around
Fireman Sullivan's neck, shall we?" Alice suggested.

The kids seemed amenable to idea. Danny wasn't
sure if he preferred Stephanie to do the deed or a four-
year-old with sticky hands and a streak of blue paint
on his chin. Neither seemed a good choice.

Stephanie's teasing eyes as she approached suggested the kid would have been the better bet.

"Maybe I ought to call the *Paseo Daily Press*,"
she said, grinning at his discomfort. "A front-page
photo of this would be great PR for the fire department."

"You pull a stunt like that and you're toast!" he
whispered through gritted teeth and forced a smile.

Her light laughter rippled around him like the rain-
bows circling the room. He caught her scent, something fresh and floral, as she leaned forward to place
the medal around his neck. Her breasts loomed in
front of him. Eye level. Tempting. Definitely not
Twiggy.

Leaning back, he tried to escape the allure of her
full figure. The rocker landed on Buttons's tail in mid-
wag. He yelped and scrambled away. The sudden
movement caught Stephanie off guard. With a cry of
alarm, she tumbled into Danny's lap. Instinctively his
arms wrapped around her.

She didn't weigh much, he thought with a rush of
conflicting emotions. She fit nicely where she had
landed but she didn't belong there. Her skin was soft,

caressable. He ought to help her up but he didn't want to let her go. Her kissable lips were enticingly close to his. His rebellious body wasn't listening to his brain, definitely had a mind of its own.

Shoving her hands against his chest, she righted herself. Her breath came fast, in tiny gasps; so did his. Her cheeks were flushed and her hair mussed, the coffee-brown curls going every which way. He wondered if she realized how she affected him. A totally inappropriate reaction given the situation. And he didn't know how she could have missed his response to her being in his lap.

With a whispered "Sorry" she stepped away from him.

Amid giggles and screams, the preschoolers had cleared the way.

Still unable to figure out quite what had happened, Danny stood, tugging Buttons to heel as a way to distract himself and get his reactions back under control.

Alice swept up beside him. "Perhaps we'd better let Fireman Sullivan put the medal around his own neck."

"Good plan," he muttered. Stephanie was still staring at him as if she'd felt the earth move. Or maybe she'd been offended by his reaction to having her in his lap. Or maybe she knew he wanted her there again without such a big audience.

Somehow they managed to make the exchange, their fingers barely brushing as she handed him the medal, which sent off a new round of sparks. He reversed his earlier conclusion. It had to be the dry air and static electricity that was giving him jolts with a high-powered charge. Not Stephanie.

"Thank you so much for coming," Alice said, her voice as soft and sweet as ice cream as he looped the ribbon around his neck.

"No problem," he lied.

"If you're not doing anything this weekend, Stephanie and I are planning to paint the kitchen on Saturday. You know, spruce up the place after the fire."

His head whipped around to nail Stephanie with a frown. "She shouldn't be painting. She's—"

"If you and some of your friends were to drop by, that might be a good idea."

He got a seriously uncomfortable feeling in his midsection. He was being manipulated. He knew it and still he couldn't figure out how to avoid the inevitable. He couldn't let Stephanie expose herself to paint fumes. Not while she was pregnant. Who knew what that would do to the baby?

Grimacing, he swallowed hard. "I'll be here."

Alice smiled in a way that suggested she'd known all along he was a sucker.

"No, wait!" Stephanie protested. "I don't want you to—"

He ignored her. "Bye, kids. Thanks for the medal." They waved to him, and he made a hasty retreat out the door with Buttons on a short leash.

Naturally Stephanie didn't leave it at that.

"Danny, wait!"

Running away wasn't an option. He'd just been

awarded a medal for bravery, hadn't he? So he halted at the fence gate. He could still make a quick getaway if she'd gotten the wrong idea about him. About *them*. There wasn't any *them*. There couldn't be.

"I don't want you to help paint the kitchen."

"You shouldn't be exposed to the fumes."

"There'll be ample ventilation."

"I doubt your father would agree with that."

"It's not my father's problem. It isn't yours, either, and I don't appreciate you trying to boss me around."

"Me?" His hand covered his chest in mock surprise. "I never bossed you around in my life. Even if I tried, you wouldn't listen."

"You've *always* tried to boss me around, ever since I was a little kid. But you're right about one thing."

He frowned. Stephanie rarely conceded he was right about anything. "What's that?"

"I don't listen. Now will you please forget about coming in to paint on Saturday?"

He considered her request. He wanted an excuse to stay away but her health and that of the baby came first. "If you won't listen to me, will you at least ask your doctor? Listen to him?"

"To her." At the sound of recorded music coming from inside the school, she glanced back over her shoulder. "All right, I guess that's fair. I'll check with my doctor."

A compromise. That felt like progress. Maybe he'd found a way out. "You'll let me know if she says no so I can help out?"

She gave a weary shake of her head. "You certainly are pushy, aren't you?"

"Yep." He grinned. "That's why the ladies find me so irresistible."

With an audible sigh, she rolled her eyes.

"Gotta go. Keep me posted, huh?"

"Sure. And, Danny, I'm sorry about what happened in there." She looked at him with her clear hazel eyes, the sparks of amber tamped down for the moment.

Danny decided to play it dumb. He knew what she was talking about. His reaction to her being in his lap. But he wasn't going to admit anything. It would take the jaws-of-life to pry the truth out of him. "It's okay. I just didn't think I deserved a medal, is all."

She tilted her head, a quirk she'd developed when she was puzzled by something.

The time was ripe for his escape before she asked any questions. "Come on, Buttons. Gotta go."

Stephanie stood on the walkway as Buttons trotted out of the gate beside Danny and they both got into his SUV. Inside the school, the children were singing "Itsy-Bitsy Spider." Stephanie felt as though she'd just been washed down the waterspout.

She couldn't have imagined the sparks that had flown between them when she'd landed in Danny's lap. In all the years they'd known each other, he'd never once given her a hint that he was attracted to her. Until today.

Not that it mattered. He'd made it pretty obvious he didn't like kids. They made him nervous. He'd been uncomfortable the whole time he'd been inside the preschool, despite the fact he'd easily handled the children's questions, and they'd warmed up to him immediately.

Very soon she'd be having a baby, who would quickly turn into a kid. Whatever his physical reaction might be to her awkward plop into his lap, Danny Sullivan wouldn't be interested in pursuing a personal relationship with her. Not in this lifetime.

Given Edgar's reaction to her pregnancy, she was all too familiar with a man's aversion to paternity.

With a weary sigh, she headed back into the school as the kids began the final chorus of "Itsy-Bitsy Spider." She'd have to find her own way back up the spout and learn how to stay there without getting washed down the next time a few raindrops came into her life.

Chapter Three

Carrying his uniform on a hanger, Danny headed into the station house shortly before the 8:00 a.m. shift change. The wide doors to the bay area yawned open revealing two fire engines, a ladder truck and a paramedic unit gleaming bright red in the overhead lights.

No hose lay stretched out drying, there was nobody hurrying to wipe down the trucks after a run. It looked as though B shift had had a quiet night.

Maybe C shift would be luckier and catch a good fire before their twenty-four hours were up.

The fire department's administrative offices occupied the first floor of the main station—a fairly new building in town—with sleeping quarters, the kitchen and dining area on the two floors above that.

Danny made for the stairs but the sound of jingling bracelets brought him up short. He winced, a premonition of doom settling over him.

"Danny, there's something I want you to take a look at."

Turning, he eyed Emma Jean Witkowsky, the station's dispatcher and resident gypsy fortune-teller,

with suspicion. As usual she was all decked out with
dangling earrings and an armful of silver bracelets.
Her long skirt swayed at her calves and she clanked
with every step she took.

"I gotta get changed before the shift starts," he
said.

"This will only take a minute. There's something
strange going on with my crystal ball. I thought
maybe you could make sense of it."

"I'm not really into crystal balls. Or fortune-
telling." Particularly Emma Jean's version, which
was invariably wrong.

She ignored his objection, shoving open the door
to Dispatch and stepping inside.

With a shrug, Danny followed her. How long could
it take to look into a stupid crystal ball and duck back
out again?

"I just bought this new ball via the Internet and I
think there's something wrong with it," she said, slipping behind the counter that separated visitors from
an array of computer terminals and phones. She
placed a globe on the counter and slowly removed the
blue silk hankie that covered it. "Tell me what you
think."

Disinterested, he glanced at the glass ball...and
nearly choked.

Looking back at him was the image of a grinning
hamster with big red lips and long eyelashes. Beside
it a typed note read, "Your love life is on the up-
swing."

Danny was torn between laughter and an urge to

throttle Emma Jean. "Thank God you haven't gotten a prediction right in the past five years."

Affronted, she widened her eyes. "I foretold Logan Strong and Janice getting together, didn't I? And Mike Gables and—"

"Enough!" He backed toward the door. "Leave me out of your fortune-telling. And for God's sake, could everybody please forget about that hamster? Next time, I'll let the damn thing suffocate."

He wouldn't, of course. Not when somebody like Stephanie made him want to revive a stupid rodent or die trying—all to impress a beautiful woman.

BY AFTERNOON, DANNY was bored out of his gourd.

Engine 62's only action so far had been to tag along on a paramedic call to old Mrs. Trumblebird, who managed to have palpitations or a wastebasket fire every week or so. Today she'd been short of breath. Mostly Danny thought she was lonely but the ambulance hauled Abigail off to the hospital anyway. She'd be pampered for a couple of days and maybe her family would visit her.

Heck of a way to spend your golden years.

After logging an hour on the stationary bike, then showering, he wandered out in back of the station. Tommy Tonka was sitting in the driver's seat of Big Red, a vintage 1930s fire engine the adolescent had helped the department restore. Today he looked glum.

"What's up, kid?"

He lifted his bony shoulders. "Nuthin'."

Danny swung up into the seat beside him. "Funny,

from the look of things, I would have guessed your best friend died.''

Head bent, shoulders slumped, the sixteen-year-old slid his hands around the steering wheel. When it came to anything mechanical, Tommy was a near genius. Personality wise, he was definitely on the slow side.

''I got dumped,'' he said.

''By that pretty redhead you brought to the Founder's Day Parade last fall?'' The two of them had ridden down Paseo Boulevard in Big Red with the Station 6 crew and their wives, Tommy looking so proud of himself Danny thought the kid might burst with it.

''Yeah. Rachel. She's dating a jock now. Varsity basketball.''

''That's rough.'' Leaning back, Danny propped one foot on the dashboard. ''So what are you gonna do about it?''

''What can I do? Heck, he's a big school hero, scores twenty points a game.'' Mimicking Danny's position, Tommy scooted lower in the seat and propped his size twelve tennis shoe against the dashboard. The laces were untied and the sole looked like it was about to come off.

''I'd bet you have a lot more between the ears than this other guy has. You can figure out a way to get her back—if you want to.''

His face flushing, which emphasized a bad case of acne, Tommy slid his gaze across to Danny. ''You know how to turn me into a jock before the spring dance?''

"Uh, that's kind of a hard one."

"Yeah, that's what I thought, too." Dejection drove his shoulders lower.

"But hey, you can't just give up if that's what it will take to get Rachel back. Nothing is impossible if you want it bad enough."

Tommy didn't look convinced.

Mentally trying to pluck a rabbit out of the hat, Danny said, "You could go out for the triathlon."

The boy's head snapped up. "You want me to do what?"

"You can swim, can't you? And ride a bike? And I know you can run." In each case, Danny gave a dispirited nod. "Then all you have to do is put them together. There's a junior division in the upcoming firefighters triathlon. You could train with me."

"I don't know. I've never been out for any kind of sport, not even Little League. My mom never had the money for fees or uniforms, stuff like that."

"It's okay. We've got weight-training equipment in the basement. We'll get you some decent shoes, and I've got an extra bike you can use. At the very least, it will keep your mind off your troubles. What have you got to lose?"

The faintest spark of hope appeared in the kid's eyes. "You think I could—"

"Damn right you could." He grinned at the boy and got a tentative smile in return. "And if I know anything about women—which I do—Rachel's gonna fall all over herself trying to get back together with you. Brains and brawn are a tough combination to beat.''

''Then, could I maybe start now?''

Suddenly the boy looked so eager, Danny almost laughed. Instead he clamped his hand on Tommy's shoulder and gave a little squeeze. ''Now sounds like a perfect time.''

Danny wasn't entirely sure what he'd gotten himself into. But he did know what it was like to be raised by a single mom. There was never enough money to go around. Pinching pennies was a way of life. And it hurt like hell not having a dad like the other kids.

For Danny, Harlan Gray had filled some of that void.

He couldn't help but wonder who would be the man Stephanie's baby would turn to.

Silently cursing the guy who had gotten Stephanie pregnant, then dumped her, Danny jumped down from the fire truck. With an effort, he battled back old memories of anger and helplessness, and a fury that made him want to punch out that stranger's lights.

''Come on, Tommy, my man. Let's see a little hustle, a little *en…thuu…siasm!*''

He jogged off ahead of the boy, into the station and down the stairs to the basement. He'd pedal another hour on the bike to bleed off his anger while Tommy worked out. Maybe, if he was lucky, he'd be able to sleep tonight without worrying about Stephanie and her baby.

SHE HAD TO STOP PEERING out the kitchen window trying to catch a glimpse of Danny.

Through her adolescent years, Stephanie had logged hours upon hours puttering in the kitchen, just far enough back from the window so he wouldn't catch a glimpse of her. Assuming he ever looked in her direction. Which he probably hadn't.

Nonetheless, she'd turned snooping on the boy down the street into an art form.

"Is something wrong out there?"

She jumped at the sound of her father behind her. "No, nothing." Her voice squeaked.

"Good, then I'm hoping it's about dinnertime."

"Coming right up." Chastising herself for her wayward thoughts, she used a hotpad to pick up the frying pan filled with Sloppy Joe mixture and carried it into the dining room where the family had always eaten their dinners when Stephanie's father was home. When he was working, her mother had served her two daughters their meals less formally in the kitchen.

"C shift is on duty tonight," her father commented idly from his place at the head of the table.

"Oh?" She went back to the kitchen to get milk for herself and water for her dad.

"I can get you a station schedule, if you'd like."

Acting unconcerned, she placed the glasses on the table. "Did I ask?"

"No. I just thought it would easier for you if you knew when to bother looking out the window to see if Danny's home."

She glared at her father, which didn't do an iota of good. The only redeeming merit of this conversation was the faint hope Danny would be too tired after twenty-four hours on duty to show up tomorrow at the preschool to help them paint over the fire and smoke damage.

By morning she knew that wasn't going to happen.

At ten minutes after eight there was a knock on the door.

"Are you ready to go?" he asked.

Dressed in ratty jeans and an old T-shirt, he looked sexy as all get out. In contrast, her ballooning blouse and baggy shorts simply made her look fat.

"Go where?"

"To the preschool. It's painting day."

"You mean you're not going to tie me to a chair and leave me here at home in order to protect me from those nasty fumes you're so worried about?"

He cocked one eyebrow, an incredibly seductive mannerism he'd perfected during his adolescent years. "Darn, I hadn't thought of that. You got any rope?"

"Oh, hush!" Barely able to suppress a smile, she swatted his arm with the back of her hand. "I could drive myself, you know."

"I figured it didn't make any sense for both of us to drive since I've gotta come back here tonight anyway. Better to save on gas."

As if an eighth of a gallon would make much difference. "What? Saturday night and no big date? You're slipping, Sullivan."

"Some of us are willing to make huge sacrifices

for the greater good.'' He glanced past her as if expecting her father to appear. "Come on, Twiggy. Time's a'wasting.''

She bristled. She really didn't need to hear that nickname again, especially when this particular twig had swollen to proportions previously unknown to humankind.

And she wasn't done growing yet.

They walked down the driveway together, and he halted at the passenger side of his SUV, blocking her way. "You did talk to your doctor like you promised, didn't you?''

"Of course.''

He cocked a brow. "And she said?''

"For the sake of my blood pressure, I should stay away from exasperating men like you.''

His rich baritone laughter wrapped around her like an old, familiar blanket on a chilly night and did something extraordinary to her insides.

And it irritated her like crazy that he could affect her so strongly after all these years.

"You don't have to come at all, you know, since the doctor said I'd be fine.''

Ignoring her comment, he played the gentleman, helping her up into his SUV—which annoyed her even more.

ALICE HAD RECRUITED HER husband, Jeffrey Tucker, to help with the painting job. A grocery store manager by trade, he was long and lanky with a receding hairline that he'd covered with a white painter's cap. Carrying a gallon can of paint in each hand, he greeted Stephanie and Danny when they arrived.

"Alice has the coffee brewing. Should be ready in a minute."

"Sounds good to me," Danny said.

"Is there more stuff in your van?" Stephanie asked, noting the familiar nine-passenger vehicle parked at the curb that the school used for field trips.

"Right. Ladders, drop cloths, rollers, the works."

Danny angled toward the van. "We'll get 'em."

Stephanie followed him, making a concerted effort not to notice his tight buns. Either bicycle riding was an excellent firming exercise or men got all the genetic breaks when it came to avoiding cottage cheese derrieres. Probably some of both.

He handed her a bundle of old drop cloths. "I don't want you climbing any ladders today."

"Oh?"

"And you need to take lots of breaks, too. I don't want you to get overtired."

"Oh, you don't, huh?" A spark of anger fed her rising temper.

"Nope." He reached for an extension ladder to slide it out of the van. "We'll have to be careful that the place is well ventilated so you—"

She clamped her hand on the ladder. "Daniel Sullivan, I have spent the past two years in a relationship with the bossiest man on the face of the earth. He told me where we would go, what I should wear and where I should shop. Half the time he ordered dinner for me as if I were a child who didn't know my own mind. And the worst thing is, I *let* him do it.'' She leveled Danny the sternest look she could manage. ''No man is going to boss me around like that again. I'm a grown woman and I can decide for myself what I'm going to climb and what I'm not.''

His eyes held hers, the most sincere, most stubborn shade of blue imaginable. ''Fine by me. Then I'll assume you're smart enough to know you shouldn't be climbing ladders in your condition.''

''I can climb—''

''For the sake of the baby.''

She wanted to argue but, of course, he was right. No way would she risk her unborn child. ''As long as you know I'm not climbing ladders because you ordered me not to. Only because of the *baby*.''

''Absolutely.'' A teasing smile threatened at the corners of his lips and his eyes began to sparkle. ''You never did anything I told you when you were a kid. Can't think why you'd start now.''

Rather than giving him the satisfaction of returning his smile—which she was sorely tempted to do—she sniffed with mock disdain. ''See that you remember that.''

''Yes, ma'am,'' he muttered as she whirled, bundle of drop cloths hugged to her chest, and marched into the preschool.

Danny watched her for a moment, taking special note of her long, firm legs, then hauled the ladder out of the van.

He'd discovered yet another reason why he'd like to get his hands on the guy who'd gotten Stephanie pregnant. He didn't like the thought that she'd cared for the guy so much that she'd forgotten how to be feisty, to talk back. To argue until she was blue in the face.

In his view, that was one of her most admirable qualities. She didn't take guff from anyone, including him.

Smiling, he carried the ladder up the walkway. Seemed to him that Stephanie was well on her way to being her old self again. She certainly seemed ready enough to give him plenty of grief. He was looking forward to sparring a few rounds with her anytime she gave him the go ahead.

Within hours, Stephanie was more than ready to take one of those breaks Danny had been so insistent upon. Alice and Jeff were struggling to paint in the close confines of the storeroom while she and Danny labored in the kitchen area. Her back ached. She had the troubling feeling her ankles had begun to swell.

Ah, the joys of pregnancy, she thought as she boosted herself up to sit on a worktable to watch the master painter.

"You missed your calling," she said.

Perched on the ladder, Danny was cutting in a swath of paint where the ceiling met the walls to make the roller work easier. "How's that?"

"You wield a mean paintbrush."

He glanced over his shoulder and grinned. "I have all kinds of talents you have yet to plumb."

Stephanie suspected that was true—and many of those talents were no doubt related to his ability to seduce women. She wasn't about to lead the conversation in that direction.

"I didn't know you were a smoke jumper. Do you still parachute for fun?"

His brush stopped in midstroke and his shoulders visibly tensed. "No. Too many memories."

Stephanie sensed she'd touched an emotional hot button. "What happened?" she asked cautiously.

He climbed down the ladder and moved it to the right a few feet, but he didn't look at her.

"They were dropping us way inside the wilderness area. Two planeloads of guys. Hotshots going after lightning-started fires. Something happened—" Resting his hand on a rung of the ladder, he shook his head. "The wind shifted just as we were bailing out. It blew us right smack into the face of the fire. Two of the guys..."

Hopping down from the table, Stephanie crossed the room to him. His shoulders shook and she placed her hand on his back, soothing him.

Visibly struggling with his memories, he fought to pull himself together. "They drifted right into a couple of trees that were already on fire. The turpentine in a pine tree turns it into a torch, the flames going maybe a hundred feet high. Even with all their protective gear on—"

"Oh, God..." Her fingers trembled. She could see what he saw, feel what he felt. A firefighter's daughter knew the awful realities of fighting a fire. The danger. The fear. What the red devil could do to a man.

"My damn canopy melted in the heat, and I hit the ground hard. And then I ran." He looked up at the ceiling, the uneven border of new paint over old, his Adam's apple working in his throat. "It's not something I'm exactly proud of."

"Shh." Instinctively she took him in her arms. Tall and strong, yet as vulnerable as a child whose invisible wounds had never healed. How many other scars did he have? she wondered. His childhood hadn't been easy. Yet somehow he'd found the strength to make the most of himself. "There wasn't anything else you could have done. You couldn't save your friends. There was no way."

"Yeah, I know." Gathering himself, he gave her a quick hug, then stepped away. "Gotta tell you, though. Seventy-five pounds of gear and I swear I set a new world's record for the quarter-mile run. I've never moved so fast in my entire life."

She recognized he was trying to lighten the mood and went along. "Maybe instead of the triathlon, we ought to sign you up for the next Olympics."

"Not much chance of that." With an easy shrug, he started up the ladder again, brush in hand.

Stephanie wished he'd hugged her a little longer. She liked the feel of his arms around her. She even liked the paint-tinged smell of him clashing with the lingering soapy scent from his morning shower.

But she reminded herself the most she could hope to have with Danny was a platonic relationship. Neighbors. Part of the extended family of firefighters. Friends who cared about each other.

Not that she'd want more than that, given her pregnant state. Or even if she wasn't pregnant, she told herself.

But she really did like the way his arms felt wrapped around her. And how her head fit so neatly resting on his shoulder at the crook of his neck. And how her palms itched to cup that tight butt of his.

She sighed and mentally swore. Her hormones must be on the fritz. Pregnancy did that to a woman, or so the book said.

Picking up the roller she'd been using, she ran it through the pan of paint. "Dad says you're the big gun on Paseo's triathlon team."

"Yeah, and every race I rededicate myself to those guys in Idaho."

She shivered. No man could outrun such a terrible memory.

Just as she'd never forget she had once placed her trust in a man who was unable to love her...or her baby.

"YOU LOOK LIKE YOU'VE BEEN infected by a severe case of white spotted fever." Painting job completed and ready to head for home, Danny opened the truck door for Stephanie.

"I always looked forward to your compliments. They're so..." She boosted herself into the seat. "...flattering to a woman's ego."

"Hey, on you, white spots are kinda cute. Like freckles."

"Wonderful." Rolling her eyes, she half turned in search of her seat belt.

Automatically Danny helped her out by grabbing the metal connector and reaching across her lap to snap it in place. For a moment, his forearm rested on her midsection, making him intimately aware of the swell of her belly. Then something poked him.

He froze and so did Stephanie.

"What was that?"

"The baby."

"He *kicked* me?"

"She kicked you. I had a sonogram last week. It's a girl."

He wanted to move away, to ignore the sudden tightening in his throat, the twist in his gut. Instead he slipped his palm across her belly, cupping her. This was real. Not a shadowy, half-formed thought that Stephanie—the pesky kid who lived down the street—was *someday* going have a baby of her own. This was *now*.

Beneath his palm, the baby moved again. A tiny foot pressing into his hand or a tight little fist.

An unfamiliar emotion filled his chest. He could barely breathe and had to clear his throat before he could speak. "Feisty as her mom, huh?"

A sheen of tears filled Stephanie's hazel eyes, dimming the flecks of gold hidden there. "With any luck, she'll come out ready to arm-wrestle you."

"Probably beat me, too."

Her teary smile nearly undid him. Without removing his hand, he leaned forward and kissed Stephanie on her temple. She'd perspired during the day, making her natural waves frizz around her face, and the strands were soft against his lips.

"You'll be a great mom, Stephanie. A great mom."

Chapter Four

The heat of his palm seeped through Stephanie's blouse to warm her belly. The sweetness of his breath swept across her damp forehead like a refreshing spring breeze.

But it was the intimacy of his touch that brought a tightness to her chest. A fierce longing she hadn't recognized she'd been harboring.

Other than herself and assorted medical personnel, Danny was the first person to feel her baby move, to acknowledge her daughter existed in more than an abstract way. In the depth of his blue eyes, she saw the same awe she experienced every day. The reflection of her own wonder that a tiny, helpless person was growing inside her.

She ached to share her amazement, her excitement with someone special. To relate each change in her body, every new sensation, the pokes and prods the baby gave her, her daughter's periodic hiccups that jiggled her tummy.

In return, she longed for someone to reassure her that her fears were unfounded. Motherhood was as natural as waking up in the morning. She and the baby would both be fine.

But she couldn't lay all of that on Danny. She wasn't carrying his baby; he wasn't responsible for either her or her daughter. He wouldn't want to be.

He'd made it pretty obvious that he wasn't comfortable around kids. They made him nervous. And unless things had changed since his high school days, he didn't lack for women in his life. No way would he want to be saddled with a pregnant woman who he still thought of as the pesky kid down the street.

No, he wouldn't want her and her baby any more than Edgar had. In their own way, they were too much alike—playboys who were too damn bossy.

Stephanie would simply have to get on with her life without that special someone. Single moms managed on their own all the time. She would, too.

"Guess we'd better get home," he said, taking a step back.

She struggled not to miss his touch, to ignore the tender ache of longing that filled her chest. "Fine by me. Dad's likely to be home soon and looking for his dinner."

His dark brows pulled together. "Don't you think you ought to take a nap or something? You had a long day."

"Evidently you haven't heard that old story about a woman's work is never done."

"Yeah, but—"

"Home, Daniel. I'm fine." Which didn't mean the

thought of a nap lacked appeal. A chance to put her feet up for a while was equally tempting.

He closed her door and walked around the truck to the driver's side.

"You and your dad still like to go up to San Francisco to take in a baseball game now and then?" he asked as he pulled the truck away from the curb.

She smiled at the memories his question brought back. "I haven't been in years. I don't think Dad has, either."

"Your, ah, boyfriend didn't enjoy sports?"

"Not likely. He was more into opera and the theater. Opening night box seats right next to the ones his parents had held for years. Formal attire. Dinner afterward at whatever place was currently in with the wealthy crowd."

"Big spender, huh?"

"Very. New Jaguar every two years. Weekend flights on the Concorde to Paris whenever the urge struck him, at least he did before the planes were grounded." Everything he did designed to sweep a woman off her feet, which is exactly what he'd done to Stephanie—to her great regret now.

Danny glanced at her. "Funny. For my money, baseball is a lot more fun than listening to some screeching soprano."

She laughed. "Let's say the experience broadened my horizons." Just as the pregnancy was broadening her hips.

"I remember your dad taking me along to Giants' games with you and your sister. It was great. You know, freezing our buns off in that cold wind coming off the bay at Candlestick Park. The Giants always managing to lose their big lead against the Dodgers and blowing the game.'' He laughed softly. ''Your dad stuffed us with popcorn and pizza and sodas until I could barely walk back to the car.''

''And I'd eat so much I'd get sick on the ride home.''

Danny shuddered. ''Yeah, I remember that, too.'' He glanced over at her and winked. ''You were such a wimp.''

''I was not!'' She huffed dramatically. Despite the car sickness, those trips had been fun. More so than a lot of the operas she'd attended. ''I simply had a sensitive stomach, not a cast-iron one like some folks I know.''

''Speaking of your sister, how's Karen doing these days? I don't see her around much.''

''Fine, I guess. Her husband's stationed in Texas now, when he's not being deployed to some hot spot around the world. She's pretty busy with the kids, I imagine.''

About the time Stephanie was graduating from college, her younger sister had announced she was getting married. The reason for the hurry-up nuptials had become apparent six months later when Christopher Malone was born. Eighteen months after that Bryana arrived.

Apparently the Gray sisters hadn't paid close enough attention in the sex education classes at Paseo

High School. They'd missed the meaning of "Just Say No."

Never once had Stephanie's father criticized either of his daughters for their slips in judgment. He simply gave them a hug and said he loved them. Pretty terrific guy.

She slid her gaze to Danny as he turned onto their street. With a father who had deserted him, he hadn't had the breaks she and her sister had enjoyed. Still, he'd made the most of what he'd been given. She'd give him credit for that.

But that didn't mean she could rely on him any more than she'd been able to rely on Edgar. Once burned, as they say, could happen to anyone. But twice burned, shame on me! Stephanie wasn't going to risk getting burned again anytime soon.

Danny pulled the truck into her driveway. "Delivered to your doorstep, madam."

Her father waved from the porch and walked down the steps. "Hello, Danny. Good to see you. How'd the painting job go?"

"Everything's under control," he replied.

To Stephanie's dismay, Danny switched off the ignition as if he were planning to stay a while. She opened her own door and hopped down.

"I'm sure Alice and Stephanie both appreciate your help." Her father reached out for Stephanie and wrapped his arm around her shoulder. "Say, why don't you stay for dinner, Danny? Stephanie's a great little cook and she could whip us up something. It'd be like old times having you at the table."

Stephanie balked. "Wait a minute."

"Steph's already worked hard enough for today," Danny said.

Mentally Stephanie exhaled a sigh of relief. Danny was going to decline the invitation.

"So why don't I go clean up," he continued, "then go by the Chinese place on Broadway and get us some take-out?"

She sputtered an objection, not that either of the men were paying attention to her. They were too involved in deciding between fried rice, chow mein and sweet-and-sour pork.

"Wait a minute!" she shouted.

They both stopped talking and gaped at her. "What?" they said in unison.

She glared at her father. "If we're having Danny for dinner," she said ever so sweetly, "maybe we ought to invite Councilwoman Anderson to join us. I'm sure she *loves* Chinese as much as I do." If her dad could do a little matchmaking—over Stephanie's objection—so could she.

Paling, her father returned her glare. "I'm not so sure—"

"That'd be great," Danny said. He tossed Stephanie a confident smile that dimpled his cheek. "You get lots more stuff when you order for four."

Inwardly Stephanie groaned. Matched against Danny *and* her father, she was a sure loser. "Would you like me to call Mrs. Anderson, or would you like to call her yourself, Dad?"

Admitting defeat, her father did an eye roll. "I'll call her," he muttered.

BACK AT HIS HOUSE, Danny had just stepped out of the shower when the phone rang. The thought that Stephanie might be calling to cancel the Chinese take-out punched him in the gut. Funny, he'd never before looked forward to fried rice with such enthusiasm.

Wrapping a towel around his waist, he picked up the phone. "Yeah."

"Yo, Sullivan. How's it going, buddy?"

Danny instantly recognized Moose Durban's voice. Friends and rivals since high school, they'd vied for everything you could name, including girls and honors on the playing field. So far the score was dead even. The tie breaker was the upcoming triathlon when Moose would represent the fire department in the neighboring town of La Verde. "Can't complain. You?"

"Hey, I'm ready to party, like always. You got plans for tonight?"

"Yeah, sort of."

"Girl-type plans?"

He pictured Stephanie, thought about the baby daughter she was carrying, and smiled. "A couple of girls, actually."

"Fat city! Bring 'em along and we'll hit some clubs. I hear they've got a hot band doing a gig down at Pismo. Let's rock."

Normally Danny would be good to go with his buddy. Party hardy, that was their motto despite their rivalry. But tonight the thought of rocking and rolling in the singles scene seemed trivial compared to spending a couple of hours with Stephanie over a few cartons of take-out. But he didn't think Moose would understand his change of heart.

"Can't do it, man." He searched for an excuse that wouldn't make him sound like a wimp. "I'm in training, you know. No booze and lots of z's."

"Come on, man. You never let a race slow you down before. Or don't you want to share the wealth? If you're squiring two chicks around—"

"It's not like that." Stephanie was definitely not a chick. Well, maybe she was cute enough to fall into that category but she had too much class. And would probably give him a tongue-lashing if he ever described her that way. Righteously so. "Let's make it another time, okay?"

"Sure, whenever."

He could hear the hurt in his friend's voice. A week ago Danny might have canceled what amounted to a family dinner to go bumming around with his buddy. He sure as hell wasn't thinking of the evening ahead of him as a date. Not by a long shot.

Stephanie was more like a little sister. Sure he cared about her, but not *that* way. And she might have had a crush on him when she was a kid, but she'd long since outgrown that. She'd moved on to much greener pastures. He couldn't help it if sometimes he reacted to her in a man-woman way. That didn't mean he had ulterior motives. It meant his hormones were working like they should. Nothing more than that.

He shifted his thoughts back to Moose. "I'll call you, man. We'll get together. I promise."

His friend didn't sound convinced as he hung up.

Danny didn't believe it either. Not really. More than once in recent years, Danny had been disturbed because Moose hadn't outgrown his need to score with every woman he dated. Now, knowing how Stephanie had been dumped the moment she announced she was pregnant, Moose's attitude bothered him even more.

"Guys ought to take some responsibility," he mumbled to himself as he went to get dressed. From his perspective, chow mein and egg rolls were sounding better and better. The perfect nutritional supplement to give him a boost in preparation for race day, less than three months away.

A HALF-DOZEN CARTONS of Chinese food sat in the center of the dining-room table on a lazy Susan, most of the containers still half full. The scent of sweet-and-sour and soy sauce hovered in the air.

Danny had gone overboard ordering enough dinner for ten people. Stephanie figured she and her father would be eating leftovers for days.

Evie Anderson, an attractive gray-haired widow in her sixties, was wearing a feminine silk blouse with a scalloped collar. She placed her fork across her plate and leaned back with a sigh. "I don't believe I could eat another bite. Everything was delicious."

"Don't forget your fortune cookie," Danny reminded her, shooting the councilwoman one of his patented grins. He'd dressed informally, in jeans and a stenciled T-shirt, which pulled tautly across his well-muscled chest. "Could be your love life is about to improve."

A tinge of extra color brightened her cheeks. "Oh, no, I'm too old for that." She glanced at Stephanie's father, no doubt in the hope Harlan would disagree with her. The poor woman had been pursuing him for ages with little encouragement from the man, which didn't seem to deter her ambition to nab him.

Harlan didn't look in Evie's direction. "I always get the fortune that bawls me out for something."

"You won't tonight," Danny assured him, passing Harlan the bag of cookies. "I made a special deal with the cookie maker—all my friends get good fortunes when I'm buying."

Harlan cracked open a cookie and pulled out the strip of paper. "See, I told you. It's the same one I always get. 'Don't forget to take out the garbage.'"

Stephanie laughed. "It's not. Let me see that."

Instead of passing her the slip of paper, he wadded up the fortune, stuffed it into his shirt pocket and handed the bag to Stephanie. "Your turn."

"That's not fair." Reluctantly she chose a cookie and passed the bag to Evie. She wasn't sure what she wanted her fortune to be beyond giving birth to a healthy baby girl. In recent months she'd been afraid to hope for too much, the fear of continued disappointment too keen to face another loss. She set the cookie aside. "I'll save this for later."

Danny shook his head. "That's against the rules.

If you don't read your fortune, it's ten years bad luck.''

"It's not," Stephanie objected.

"I'll read mine," Evie said, breaking open her cookie and squinting at the tiny piece of paper. "Oh, dear, the print is so small I can't see it. I left my glasses in the other room. It's so dreadful to be vain, don't you know?''

"Let me." Danny took the paper from her. "It says, 'Golden Lotus Cookie Company.' ''

"Not that side, young man." Evie giggled a surprisingly girlish laugh. "The *other* side."

"Oh, right." He grinned and read, "'Your heart will soon know happiness.' ''

"How nice. Don't you think so, Harlan?''

"It probably means you're going to get elected to another term on the city council. The mayor will love it.''

"Pshaw." She made a dismissive gesture with her hand. "What can you do with a man who doesn't have a romantic bone in his body?''

No one responded to her rhetorical question.

"Here's my fortune," Danny said. "'The race goes to the swift.' Perfect. The triathlon is in the bag.''

"Excellent." Harlan dropped his broken cookie onto this plate and brushed his hands together. "I'll send out a notice to the other cities telling them they don't have to enter a team. The trophy will stay in Paseo.''

Lifting his brows, Danny eyed Stephanie. "Can't

put it off any longer, Ms. Gray. Let's hear what your fortune says.''

Knowing he'd keep after her until she gave in, Stephanie snapped open the cookie. The fortune refused to come out easily, and she had to break the hard shell into little pieces. She opened the paper and silently read, *Look to your friend for the love you seek.*

Her head snapped up. Bright blue eyes snared her from across the table, and a little smile teased at the corners of Danny's lips.

Dear heaven! He couldn't know what the fortune said. He wouldn't *want* to know. And he certainly wouldn't have planted a fortune like this one for her to open. In any case, the whole idea was ludicrous. She didn't believe in fortune-telling of any kind. And there was no reason why her heart was pumping about two hundred beats per second at the mere suggestion Danny could or would fill the void in her life.

''Well?'' her father asked. ''Are you going to share the bad news with us?''

Abruptly she broke out of her trance, closing her hand around the slip of paper. ''It says if I don't get the dishes done soon you won't get the garbage taken out on time.''

''Whoa! Wait a minute,'' Danny complained.

Shoving back from the table, she picked up her plate and her father's without meeting Danny's gaze. Then she fled to the kitchen. No way would she reveal the contents of her fortune to Danny or anyone else.

Nor would she dwell on wishful thinking.

She heard Danny's unmistakable footsteps follow her into the kitchen.

"Here, let me take care of that." He stacked the two plates he was carrying on the counter and took the other two away from her before she had a chance to follow suit. "You should be resting with your feet up."

Her jaw clenched. "My feet are just fine."

Taking her by her shoulders, he tried to turn her back toward the dining room. She didn't budge. Desperately she ignored the gentle strength of his hands, his closeness, the pulse she saw beating at the base of his throat. And her own unwelcome response to being near enough to catch the fresh scent of soap on his skin.

He tipped her chin up, forcing her to look into his eyes. "What's wrong, Twiggy? Was your fortune that bad?"

"Don't call me that." The words ached in her throat, her voice barely audible past the lump of forgotten dreams. "I'm not a skinny little kid anymore."

"I didn't call you that because you were skinny." Lightly he ran his thumb over her lips. "I called you Twiggy because you reminded me of a twig planted in the ground that would one day grow into a beautiful, stately tree. Which is exactly what you've done. Except you're a woman, of course."

The press of tears suddenly burned at the back of her eyes. Hormones, she told herself. "You're just making that up to make me feel better."

"Nope. I wouldn't lie about something so important."

A delicious shiver sent gooseflesh racing down her spine. "Guys lie about a lot of things."

"Only about dumb stuff, and then mostly to impress each other. Like how many women they've—"

"I don't think I want to hear this."

His lips twitched with the threat of a smile. "Good, 'cause I wouldn't want to impress you too much."

"Not much chance of that." She swatted at his arm but he didn't let her go. "If you want to be helpful, go bring in the leftovers so I can put them in the refrigerator."

"Only if you'll tell me what your fortune really said."

"It said to beware of a wolf in sheep's clothing, particularly if his name is Danny."

He barked a laugh. "See, I told you that cookie maker was one smart fellow."

She managed to scoot away from him just as Evie walked into the kitchen.

"Here you young people are. Before I leave, I wanted to thank you for inviting me to dinner."

Guilt sent the heat of a blush racing to Stephanie's face. "We're glad you could come."

"I hope you're both planning to help out at the city's Spring Fling Carnival next weekend. We need all the volunteers we can get."

"Of course," Stephanie agreed, recalling the fun of annual visits to the carnival as a kid. "I'd be happy to help but I don't know—"

"Not to worry, my dear." Evie beamed her vote-garnering smile. "I already took the liberty of penciling your name in for the face-painting booth. For the children, you know. I hope that's all right."

"Perfect. I'd love to do that."

"I'll have someone call you." She glanced at Danny. "As for you, young man, given your recent adventures, I'd say the kissing booth would be an ideal spot for you."

Danny sputtered. "No, ma'am, I really don't think—"

"What don't you think?" Stephanie's father asked, coming into the kitchen with cartons of leftovers in hand.

"Mrs. Anderson asked me to—"

"She's typecasting us for the Spring Carnival," Stephanie said, ignoring a sudden surge of jealousy that twisted through her chest. "She wants Danny to work at the kissing booth."

Her father popped open the refrigerator and set the cartons inside. "Sounds reasonable to me."

"Chief, I'd rather not—"

"You could help out at the kissing booth, too, honey bunch."

"Dad! I'm six months pregnant! Who would want to kiss—"

"I'll work the kissing booth," Danny said in a hurry. "Stephanie would be better at face painting."

She glared at him. "So you agree no man would want to kiss me."

"I didn't say that."

"You certainly inferred it. And I notice you didn't refuse the kissing job for long, did you? I'm sure you'll make loads of money for the recreation program."

"It's a good cause," her father commented. "If we can keep kids off the streets—"

"It wasn't my idea to work the kissing booth."

"Now, now, children." Evie patted Danny on the cheek. "I'm sure the two of you will work out your differences."

"Differences?" Danny questioned.

"I know you'll come around and do the right thing by Stephanie."

Confusion clouded his face. "Right thing?"

"Marry her, of course. With the baby coming and all, I'm sure you'll want to make an honest woman of her, as we used to say."

Stephanie gasped. "No, Mrs. Anderson, you must have misunderstood. Danny isn't—"

"I'm definitely not," he agreed with a little too much haste.

"Now don't you worry, either of you. My dear, sweet Albert always said most things worked out for the best if you just gave them enough time." She smiled maternally at Stephanie. "Thank you again for suggesting Harlan invite me. Lovely evening."

Evie's leap to the wrong conclusion left Stephanie immobile and nearly speechless. "Yes, ma'am."

"I'll walk you out, Evie," Harlan offered, ushering her back toward the dining room.

Motionless, Danny stared after them for a long moment. "I'll bring in the rest of the leftovers," he mumbled.

"Danny?"

He halted on the way out the door. "What?"

"I'm sorry about Mrs. Anderson. It never occurred to me someone would think—"

"Your dad knows the truth, doesn't he?"

"Of course."

"Then forget it. The councilwoman's wheels are usually a little wobbly. It doesn't mean anything."

Stephanie wasn't at all confident the misunderstanding could be shrugged off so easily. Others might reach the same conclusion about her baby's paternity if she was seen with Danny regularly, and his denials wouldn't carry much weight. That wouldn't be fair to him. It might even damage his social life, of which she was sure he had plenty. And she hated that the thought bothered her so much.

She couldn't even bring herself to contemplate Danny spending hours working at the kissing booth, and probably enjoying every moment. That thought hurt, too.

She was even more troubled later that evening when, unable to sleep, she found herself in the kitchen peering out the window toward Danny's darkened house. *Spying* on him, not that there was anything to see.

Sighing, she realized she needed to get on with her life. Relying on her father's support, living in his house, wasn't going to cut it. She needed to get a permanent job. A place of her own, preferably well out of sight of Danny Sullivan's house where she wouldn't be constantly reminded of her adolescent fantasies.

Still, she couldn't quite forget the one positive revelation that evening—Danny thought she'd grown into a stately, beautiful woman.

It wasn't true, of course. Edgar had pointed out more than once that she wasn't movie-star gorgeous. Attractive but ordinary were his words.

Catching her lower lip between her teeth, she wondered if it would be foolish to trust Danny's judgment instead of the man's verdict who had fathered her child then rejected both Stephanie and the baby she carried.

Chapter Five

Early the next morning, Danny knocked on Stephanie's back door.

He'd been stunned by Mrs. Anderson's suggestion that he was the father of Stephanie's baby. Heaven knew he wasn't anybody's candidate for Father of the Year but he sure as hell wouldn't have turned his back on a woman who was going to have his baby. Not like his own dad had walked out on him and his mother.

So he'd spent a sleepless night trying to figure out what to do about Stephanie's situation.

Harlan Gray would make a terrific grandpa. But Stephanie and her baby needed someone to do the things a dad ought to do. In the absence of anyone else volunteering for the job, Danny would elect himself.

Which was why he was standing at her door wondering why no one was answering. He rapped his knuckles on the door again.

The curtain on the kitchen window shifted and hazel eyes peered out at him.

"Come on, slug-a-bed, up and at 'em," he called to Stephanie.

"What do you want?"

"It's time for your daily walk."

There was a brief pause and then the door flew open. "My what?"

He looked her up and down, admiring her short flannel nightie with a bright yellow Snoopy on the front. Her tousled hair and heavy-lidded eyes made him think of the way she would look after a good night of sex.

A smile curled his lips. "You're looking particularly seductive this morning."

"No, I'm not. And the operative word there is *morning. Early* morning. What are you doing here?"

"I've been reading up on the Internet about pregnancy and what an expectant mother is suppose to do, like get lots of exercise."

She eyed him incredulously. "You told me yesterday I was supposed to rest. Now you want me to—"

"They recommend daily walks. At least a half hour."

"At the crack of dawn on a Sunday morning? No, thanks."

She started to close the door but he shoved his foot in the crack. "I've got a training date later with Tommy Tonka from the station house. He's going to enter the triathlon so he can impress some girl. Which is why you and I have to do our walk now."

"I don't remember turning you into my personal trainer."

He pushed his way into the house. "Well, this is how I see things. You don't have a man around—except your dad, who doesn't count in this case—so somebody has to do all the stuff a husband and about-to-be father would do for you."

Her eyes widened and she took a step back. "*All* the stuff—"

"The important things, like making sure you eat right, take your vitamins, exercise properly."

"You're out of your mind!"

Harlan Gray appeared at the doorway, hair mussed, his robe only half on. "What's going on?"

"I'm here to take Stephanie for a walk. Exercise is important for pregnant women."

"Okay, but could you keep the racket down? I'm trying to get some sleep." He yawned.

"Right, Chief."

"Have a nice walk, honey bunch." Sleepily Harlan turned and walked back down the hallway toward his bedroom.

"Dad!" Stephanie wailed.

"Shh. Your dad needs his rest. Go throw on some clothes, and we'll get out of here."

She nailed him with a look that was meant to fry him but they both knew, one way or another, he'd win this little battle. When he made up his mind about something, he didn't give up easily.

And as of right now he'd decided to be Stephanie's pseudohusband, her baby's surrogate dad. Until a better choice came along, they were stuck with him.

MONDAY AFTERNOON STEPHANIE lifted the last of the junior-size chairs onto the play table so she could sweep up the day's debris from underneath. The preschoolers had left a half hour ago, and it was about time for her to go home, too.

She swept the floor, dumped the trash, then went to find Alice, who was doing some paperwork in her office.

"Have you got a minute?" she asked.

Alice looked up from her cluttered desk. "Sure. What's up?"

Picking up a pile of magazines and papers from the one spare chair in the room, Stephanie placed them on the floor and sat down. "I know you hired me on a temporary basis until your regular teacher comes back from maternity leave but I've been wondering if you might have a permanent spot for me."

"Oh, I'm sorry. I promised Anna Marie she could have the job back when she was ready to return to work. And truly, I don't have the budget for two aides."

"I was afraid of that."

Alice's gray eyes assessed her sympathetically. "Even if I could hire you permanently, you don't have any Early Childhood Education units, which is something I normally require of my employees. Anna Marie has her A.A. degree."

"I expected to have a career in commercial art, not teaching. But things have changed and frankly, I need some sort of a permanent job so I can move out on my own."

A frown stitched across Alice's usually smooth forehead. "It's not going well at your dad's house?"

"Dad's been wonderful." Assuming she didn't count his matchmaking efforts or the presence of an irritatingly bossy man who was too sexy for his own good. A man who lived right down the street and had the nerve to try to take over her life. "I'd just prefer a little more independence."

"I can understand that, though with the baby coming…" She left the thought hanging in the air. "Aren't there any commercial art jobs here in town? I remember how enormously talented you were all through school."

"For all the good that does me. Paseo del Real isn't exactly the advertising capital of the world." Which was one of the major reasons she'd moved away in the first place.

"No, I suppose not." She shook her head. "I'm sorry, Stephanie. You know I'd hire you if I could. You're wonderful with the children."

Stephanie pushed herself to her feet. "It was worth asking anyway. If you hear of any job openings, let me know. I'm not in a position to be real fussy."

"You might try the school district. They might have an opening for an art teacher." Distractedly, Alice glanced down at the heap of papers on her desk and gave an absent wave of her hand. "I'm sure you'll find something."

At the moment, Stephanie wasn't nearly that confident.

Still troubled about her lack of independence,

Stephanie left the preschool, closing the door firmly behind her.

She had enough savings to pay her doctor bills and for first and last month's rent on an apartment but the kicker would be the ongoing expense. For that she'd need a job. Thus far, Edgar hadn't offered a single penny's worth of assistance. He didn't deny he was the baby's father; he simply ignored the situation. She couldn't rely on him for help. Nor did she want to.

Without a decent job, though, the hope of moving out on her own was no more than a pipe dream.

Meanwhile, she'd begun to dread Danny's days off and the walks she was sure he'd insist upon. The exercise might be good for her muscle tone but strolling side by side with Danny was darn hard on her heart rate.

She'd definitely target the school district for her job-hunting efforts.

THE CITY SPRING FLING Carnival was a noon-to-midnight event at the regional park with Ferris wheel rides, whirligigs and game booths for old and young alike. Bands played all day long from a stand set up near the baseball diamond. The scent of barbecued steaks and red beans filled the air along with the smell of popcorn and cotton candy. As the night progressed there would be fireworks and a dance contest.

Stephanie dabbled a smiling clown's face on the cheek of an adorable five-year-old boy. His older sister had opted for a yellow-and-white daisy.

Across the way, the kissing booth taunted her with

its hand-lettered sign Champion Smoocher—$1 Per Kiss. All afternoon she'd watched every female in the entire city over the age of six plunk down their money for one of Danny's kisses.

She didn't need to check her paint pots to know she was green with jealousy. Darn it all, he didn't have to look so happy with his volunteer assignment.

With a sigh, she turned to the next child in line. "What will it be, honey?"

Before the youngster could answer, a teenage girl tapped her on her shoulder. "At the volunteer booth they said I should relieve you, ma'am."

She winced. She wasn't *that* much older than the adolescent. "Thanks."

Setting aside her paintbrush, she flexed her fingers, then stood, stretching and arching her back. She'd been sitting a long time. Renewed circulation made her legs tingle. What she needed was a nice long walk.

Perversely her feet took her only as far as the opposite row of booths where Danny was all puckered up for a trio of giggling high school girls.

He pecked the last one quickly on her lips, gave her long, blond hair an affectionate tug and favored her with one of his indelible smiles. "Be good, sweetheart."

The volume of giggles increased, and the girls ran off. "He is *so* hot!" one of them tittered.

Stephanie wanted to throw up.

"Your reputation has certainly preceded you," she said instead.

He shot her a dimpled grin that was even warmer than the one he'd given the girls. "Must be all that experience I got with your school's hamsters."

She rolled her eyes.

"You had quite a crowd around your booth most of the day. Guess you made a bundle, huh?"

"About half as much as you have with all your repeat customers."

"Yeah, well, I couldn't get rid of 'em, you know?"

He didn't have to look so pleased about it, she thought, gritting her teeth. "I'm going to go get something to eat. I'll see you around."

He snared her wrist before she could step away. "Wait for me. My relief ought to be here soon and we can go together."

His grip was both strong and gentle, as tempting as his full, generous lips. If she wasn't careful, she'd be putting her own money on the line for one of his kisses. That was something she couldn't afford to do.

"Hey, Sullivan, if she doesn't want to kiss you, it's against the rules to make her."

Startled by the arrival of a member of Danny's engine crew, she tried to pull away. He wouldn't let her go.

"Wells, for the first time in your life, your timing is perfect," Danny said. "I'm outta here. The lady and I have a date for some barbecued steak." Without releasing her wrist, he agilely hopped over the booth's low railing.

The firefighter waggled his dark brows. "No need to hurry back. I've got everything under control here.

Have a good time. Unless your lady friend would like to be my first customer.''

Ignoring his buddy, Danny slid his arm around Stephanie's waist, sweeping her away from the kissing booth and the competition. "Now then, I'm starved. I've been smelling that barbecue all afternoon.'' And steak wasn't the only thing he was hungry for, either.

Every time he'd looked up today, he'd seen Stephanie across the way, laughing with the little kids, touching them, smiling at them. He'd wanted to be on the receiving end of her smiles.

And he'd wanted Stephanie on the receiving end of one of his kisses. Not just a little peck like the ones he'd been giving the cadre of adolescents that had crowded his booth, but a full fledged, no-holds-barred kiss.

The kind of kiss a man gives a woman.

Not a public kiss, either, in front of half the town of Paseo. A private kiss the way it ought to be done.

"Could you slow down?" Stephanie complained. "I'm not up to a power hike today, and I'm sure they'll have plenty of steak left by the time we get there."

"I know a shortcut." He angled her into a narrow alley between two red-and-white-striped tents, one of them where Emma Jean, bangles and beads at full sway, was trying to entice folks to have their fortunes told for five dollars a shot. Danny wanted Stephanie away from all the prying eyes of carnival goers, particularly those of Emma Jean and her crystal ball.

Rounding a corner to the most private place he could find, he halted and turned Stephanie to him. "There's been something I've wanted to do all afternoon."

She arched her brows with suspicion. "What?"

"This." Without asking for permission, he covered her mouth with his. He heard a gasp of surprise, then her lips relaxed, softly molding to his. He gentled his touch, sketching the curve of her lips with his tongue. Tasting her flavor, a combination of sweetness and spice, exploring possibilities, delving deeper as she opened for him.

The noise of the milling crowd dimmed, the screams from the Ferris wheel were muted by the thud of his heart. His awareness focused entirely on the kiss. On Stephanie, and how she felt in his arms. The press of her breasts against his chest. The slight swell of her tummy as he pulled her closer. The flex of material as he slid his palm across the back of her colorful T-shirt top.

This kiss was different than any he had experienced. Not carnal. Far sweeter than he was used to and achingly filled with wanting. His or hers, he couldn't be sure which and was afraid to speculate.

He wasn't a man who made commitments. That's what she needed. But his genetic makeup, his father's legacy, didn't lend itself to forever afters. He'd never expected it to happen. Didn't think it could now no matter how much a part of him might want otherwise. He'd certainly never considered the possibility before.

He groaned, low and throaty, and lifted his head.

Slowly she opened her eyes and drew a shuddering breath. Her pupils were dilated, her cheeks flushed.

"Wow," she said softly. "That's gotta be worth more than a buck."

"For you, Twiggy, no charge."

For a moment, she simply looked up at him, myriad unreadable emotions flitting through her hazel eyes. Then she drew herself back, her spine straightening. "I thought you said you were hungry."

"I still am, but I'll settle for some barbecued steak. For now."

She cocked her head. "I'm sure food will cure whatever ails you."

SITTING AT A PICNIC TABLE near the bandstand where a children's dance troupe was performing, Stephanie picked at her plate of steak, beans and wilted lettuce salad.

Something had changed between her and Danny, and not so subtly. He sat a little closer than usual, their arms brushing despite the fact there was plenty of room at the table. He looked at her differently, his gaze somehow possessive. If anything, he'd become more bossy than before, insisting she take an extra slice of steak *for the baby*. He was driving her crazy.

She never should have let that kiss happen.

He'd caught her off guard but she still could have objected. Shoved him away. Screamed for help.

But no, she'd given into the delicious surprise of his lips on hers. She'd spent a dozen years imagining what it would be like to kiss Danny Sullivan and hadn't come close to envisioning the curl-your-toes reality.

Damn, she was in deep trouble.

"Pretty good, huh?" he mumbled with his mouth full.

"Wondrous." She sighed.

He shot her a look, his blue eyes narrowing. "I don't know that I'd call the steak *wondrous*. I mean, I've probably had better but for a picnic, it's okay."

She blinked. "Oh, no, that's not what I meant. I was thinking about—" She clamped her mouth shut before she stuck her foot in it clear down her throat.

Laying his plastic fork down on his paper plate, he turned sideways to face her. "Are you all right? You're not eating much."

"My appetite's a little off, I suppose." Confusion could do that to a woman.

"Maybe you got too much sun." He placed the back of his hand on her forehead. "You look flushed."

"I'm fine, really." Shaking off his hand, she scooped up a forkful of beans. "See, I'm eating." Swallowing, however, appeared to be a more difficult task than she recalled.

Whatever would she do if she fell for Danny for real? Not just an adolescent crush but something far more serious. He'd always been a playboy, the tempting bad boy in high school who had grown into a studly firefighter. A man who charmed the ladies at bachelor auctions but didn't know the meaning of commitment. She'd already fallen for that kind of man once and been burned.

She'd be twice a fool to go there again.

Gagging down the forkful of beans, she determinedly stabbed a bite of steak. One kiss meant nothing. A blip on the radar screen of life. She'd get over it. She'd have to because that single kiss wouldn't lead anywhere she wanted to go. Whatever Danny might feel for her, it had nothing to do with long-term commitment.

After studying her for a moment more, he went back to eating his own meal.

"After we're finished, you want to go try out the Ferris wheel?" he asked a minute or two later.

She glanced over her shoulder at the circling wheel, not a big one by amusement park standards but fine for a small-town carnival. At twilight they had turned on the lights and the wheel's neon frame sparkled in red, green and blue. From the top there would be a nice view of downtown Paseo del Real—a romantic view if you were snuggling with a—

Forcefully she put the thought aside. "I probably ought to get on home."

"What? You mean you're not going to let me win a teddy bear for you by throwing baseballs at milk bottles that are filled with concrete?"

"They are?"

"Always seemed like it to me when I was a kid. Those suckers are damn hard to knock over, particularly when you're trying to impress a girl."

In spite of herself, she smiled. "That's okay. I

don't really need a teddy bear anyway.'' Nor did she need him to impress her any more than he'd been doing for the past dozen years or so.

His gaze dropped to her midsection and he spoke softly. ''I could give it to your baby.''

His words brought the threat of tears to her eyes. A gift for her daughter. The sweetness of the thought clogged her throat. ''You don't have to—''

Nearby a woman screamed. ''Help! My husband! He can't breathe!''

Danny was on his feet and moving before Stephanie entirely registered the emergency. He'd spotted the frantic woman two tables over pounding her fist on her elderly husband's back, crying his name.

Wrenching the man from his wife's grasp, Danny hauled him upright, wrapped his arms around the man's chest, applying a Heimlich maneuver which sent the victim into a coughing spasm. Gently Danny lowered the gentleman back to a sitting position on the picnic bench. He waved off the onlookers who gathered around and spoke calmly to the victim and his wife.

Minutes later the couple stood and left the picnic area. Danny returned to where Stephanie waited for him.

''*Now* I'm impressed,'' she said as he sat down beside her.

''Didn't your dad tell you? Us firefighter types arrange emergencies like that on purpose so we can impress the girls.'' He shrugged. ''All in the line of duty, of course.''

She sent a sharp elbow into his ribs. "Yeah, right."

He laughed. "Well, it would be a good plan if we could work it out."

"Is the gentleman okay?"

"Seems to be. He choked on a bite of steak, as I suspected. But you always have to worry about broken ribs with the Heimlich. I told the wife that if he had any chest pain she ought to take him to emergency."

Unable to stop herself, she palmed his cheek. Growing serious, she said, "You did good, Danny. Dad would be pleased."

He closed his hand around her wrist. "I spent a lot of years hoping to please your dad. After my old man took off, he was the closest thing I had to a father. There isn't anything I wouldn't do for him."

Somewhere in the back of her mind, a niggling voice wondered if Danny was being so attentive out of a misdirected sense of obligation to her father. The thought was so troubling, the possibility that Danny would take loyalty that far so real, her stomach roiled.

"I think I'd better go."

Over the loudspeakers, the announcer introduced a new band that had taken center stage and invited everyone to join in with a little country two-stepping.

"Hey, you can't go yet." On his feet in a flash, Danny pulled her to hers. "You see before you the all-time Texas cham..pi..on—" he dragged out the word dramatically "—two-stepper this side of Dallas. Or at least this side of Pismo Beach." He whirled her out onto the wooden dance floor that had been set up on the baseball infield.

"Danny, I can't."

"Sure you can. If you don't know the steps, just follow me."

She was helpless to do otherwise. With his arm around her waist, he was too commanding, too determined to resist. He caught the rhythm of the music and infected her. She hadn't danced in months, maybe years, but her feet found the steps, matching his perfectly just as earlier their lips had fit together as though made for that sole purpose.

More dancers filled the floor. Teenage girls with their lithe bodies and awkward boyfriends, couples in their senior years showing the grace that comes from dancing with their partners for decades, and younger pairs who were just starting out together. Near the bandstand, children bounced a cadence of their own or rode their father's shoulders.

Stephanie recalled all the years she'd hung out around Danny's house watching him repair his assorted cars or tossing a football with his buddies and dreaming of this moment. She was breathless by the time the band slowed the pace, and it wasn't entirely because of exertion.

"Hey, you're pretty good," Danny said, easing her into his arms and matching his steps to the more sedate rhythm.

"I'd almost forgotten how much I love to dance."

His blue eyes assessed her. "The baby's okay with that much exercise?"

"Aerobics are good for a woman's circulation, I'm told."

The crowd on the dance floor had thinned, and a couple Stephanie recognized two-stepped over to them. Jay Tolliver worked with Danny at Station 6 and his wife Kim was a nighttime talk-show host on the local public radio station. Stephanie had met them both the day firefighter families had gotten together to paint the house of Janice Gainer, the widow of yet another firefighter. That's how it went in the department; the firefighters were like brothers who helped each other whenever they could.

Jay shot a grin at Danny. "Wells claims they tossed you out of the kissing booth 'cause you didn't have any takers."

"No way, but I bet he's been the loneliest guy in the park since he took over."

They both laughed.

Kim said, "Good to see you again, Stephanie. You're visiting your father?"

"Uh, not exactly. I've moved back home." At least until she could find a place of her own.

"I'm sure your dad is pleased about that." Kim's smile was genuine, the scar she'd acquired when struck by falling debris during an earthquake two years ago had faded and become less conspicuous. Pity the injury had destroyed her budding television career but she looked happy enough to be in Jay's arms.

"And wouldn't you know Sullivan would latch on to the boss's daughter as soon as she came back to town,'' Jay said. "Looking for a promotion, are you, buddy?''

Stephanie flushed.

Kim gave her husband a light swat on the arm. "That wasn't a very nice thing to say.''

"I was only teasing. I meant, she's the prettiest girl on the dance floor and it figures Sullivan would—''

"*She's* the prettiest?'' Kim questioned.

It was Jay's turn to blush. "What I meant was—''

"Leave it alone,'' Danny warned. "The hole you're digging is getting deeper by the minute.''

"Yeah, you're right.'' He brushed a kiss to his wife's forehead. "This is no time for me to get myself in the doghouse. We're going to have a baby.'' From Jay's smile, he was already a proud papa.

"Hey, congratulations to the both of you. That's terrific,'' Danny said. "Stephanie's pregnant, too.''

Kim's surprised gaze dropped to Stephanie's tummy and then to Danny. "That's wonderful. I hadn't heard the two of you were—''

"He's not the father,'' Stephanie quickly said.

"Oh.'' Nonplused, Kim was clearly at a loss for words.

Distressed, Stephanie stepped away from Danny. "It's really time for me to get on home. Good to see you both.''

Her emotions on a roller-coaster ride, she turned and fled.

Chapter Six

Danny jogged after her, weaving his way through the crowd. "Stephanie, wait up."

She kept on walking toward the well-lighted parking lot, her short, sassy hair bouncing with each step. Stubborn woman.

He could be just as determined.

He sidled up beside her and fell into step. "You want to tell me what's got your panties all twisted in a knot?"

"It should be obvious."

"Hey, I'm a guy, not a mind reader. Give me a clue."

She halted so abruptly he sailed past her a step or two and had to backtrack. "Everyone from the city council to your firefighter buddies think you're the father of my baby. Doesn't that bother you?"

"Not particularly. Should it?"

"I'm sure the next time you ask some woman out and she hears the rumor—the *false* rumor—about your paternity, it's going to bother *her*."

He shrugged. He hadn't been dating anyone special

lately. Hardly been dating at all, for that matter, and didn't have anybody in mind he wanted to ask out.

Except Stephanie. The thought popped into his head, startling him.

"Guess that would be her problem, not mine."

"Well, it bothers me." Whirling, she marched across the parking lot.

Following at a slower pace, he jammed his hands into his jacket pockets and frowned. *Dating Stephanie,* now that was a new concept. Going to movies together, hanging out at the beach, taking bike rides up the coast.

Kissing her.

He reached her car as she slid into the driver's seat, and he held the door open so she couldn't close it in his face. "Why would it bother you so much if I was the father of your baby? I'm not such a bad guy."

"I didn't mean you were a bad person. It's just that—" She slipped the key into the ignition and turned it. All she got was a click.

"You wouldn't want to have my baby."

"I didn't say that, either." She tried the key again with the same result. "I don't like the idea of somebody else getting blamed for my own stupidity."

He dropped down to his haunches beside the car. Instinctively he slid his hand across the swell of her belly. "Then under other circumstances you wouldn't mind having my baby?"

A shudder rippled through her, a reaction to his touch, not the baby moving. A *good* reaction, as though she enjoyed it.

"Not much chance of that since you've always thought of me as a pest."

At the moment, he wasn't thinking that at all. Instead he was considering the woman she had become—sexy in a mature feminine way. Maternal. Caring. Intelligent and creative. A woman with a problem. A pregnant woman he'd really like to kiss again.

She turned the key. When still nothing happened, she sighed and leaned her head on the steering wheel. "My battery's dead."

"Nope. Sounds like the starter solenoid to me." Standing, he offered her his hand. "Come on, I'll give you a ride home."

"I'll call for a tow."

"It's nine o'clock on a Saturday night. Assuming you could get someone to tow you, you couldn't get it fixed tonight anyway." He reached across her into the car, pulled the key from the ignition and stood back. Granted, the battery connectors could have worked loose and that was the problem, not the solenoid going bad, but he didn't want the breakdown solved that easily. "You've had a long day, Twigs. Let's get you home so you can get some rest."

"You're being bossy again."

"Yep, that's my nature."

She wanted to argue some more. He could see it in the stubborn tilt of her jaw, the rigid set of her shoulders. He staved off the argument by taking her arm and gently tugging her from the car.

"I'll help you get it fixed tomorrow, okay?"

Surrendering at last, she nodded. "I need to be able to get to work on Monday."

"No problem. You'll be there with bells on to greet all your little rug rats. If worse comes to worse, you can use my wheels, and I'll bike to the station house."

Meanwhile, Danny needed to give a lot of thought to the day's revelations—the fact that he liked Stephanie a lot more than he should for a man who didn't believe in commitment.

DEFINITELY DÉJÀ VU.

How many times had Stephanie hung around Danny's yard while he was working on his or a buddy's car, his head inside the engine compartment, his firm, rounded buns neatly framed between the fender and hood? Too many to count, she knew, and she shouldn't be here now admiring the view she remembered so well.

He and his young friend Tommy Tonka had hooked her car up to a towing cable this morning and hauled it to Danny's driveway. Between trips to the autoparts store, they'd been puttering with it ever since, and she'd spied on them from her kitchen window until she couldn't stand it any longer. She'd pulled on an old Paseo high school sweatshirt as protection against the cool spring breeze and strolled across the street.

"Are you two sure you know what you're doing?" she asked.

"Tommy's a genius when it comes to mechanical stuff."

"We've almost got it licked, ma'am."

Neither head appeared from beneath the hood, only their disembodied voices.

"Are you sure I shouldn't have it towed to a garage tomorrow? That might be easier." And quicker, she suspected.

"Too expensive," Danny mumbled. "We'll be done here in a minute."

"Yeah, but will my car run?"

Danny's head popped up, a streak of grease crossing his forehead at a rakish angle. "You gotta learn to have a little faith, sweetheart. It's hard on a man's ego when you doubt him."

"Like your ego needs a boost?"

"Not mine. It's Tommy here I'm worried about. I wouldn't want you to scar the lad with your skepticism."

She sputtered a laugh. Danny Sullivan was an unrepentant rake. Worse, she loved his arrogance and ought to know better.

Glancing up, she saw her father crossing the street.

"What's the problem?" he asked.

"The solenoid died," Danny answered.

All three masculine heads dropped out of sight beneath the car hood. It was a genetic thing, no doubt associated with the Y-chromosome in the way male-pattern baldness was. Men bonded under car hoods in a ritual much like slumber parties for females. The guys didn't have to know any more about cars than the girls did about sex, but both subjects became the endless topic of conversation.

Sighing, Stephanie folded her arms and waited for the participants to emerge from their ceremonial rite of passage.

Her father reappeared first. "I'd like to ask a favor of you, Danny."

"Whatever I can do, Chief." He straightened and wiped his hands on a cleaning rag.

"I got word yesterday the high-level disaster training the city is sending me to in Washington D.C. has been switched. It starts next week, which means I'm going to miss the childbirth classes I promised Stephanie I'd attend with her so I could be her coach during delivery."

"Oh, Dad…"

"So I wondered if you'd handle that for me."

Danny's jaw went visibly slack and his eyes widened.

Stephanie's panic was as real as the similar emotion Danny was no doubt experiencing. "We'll do a later session, Dad. It'll be fine."

"You need to get it done before that baby of yours decides to show up. There isn't another class scheduled at the hospital—"

"I'll get a friend to come with me."

"Who?" both men asked in unison.

As though trying to be invisible, Tommy remained out of sight with his head under the hood.

"I don't know. Maybe Mary Ellen—" A high school friend who still lived in town.

"Doesn't she have three children now?" her dad asked. "Seems to me it would be difficult for her to promise she'd be there when the time came."

"Well, Danny couldn't, either," she countered. "He might be working a shift, or even in the middle of fighting a fire. He couldn't just drop everything the moment I went into labor."

"The guys do it all the time," Danny said, finally finding his voice. "I mean, the married guys take the classes with their wives and then when the time comes we cover for 'em. You know, somebody works a couple of hours overtime. We juggle shifts. Whatever it takes. It's no big deal."

Harlan patted his protégé on the back. "I knew you wouldn't mind."

"But *I* mind," Stephanie complained. "Just because he feels obligated to *you* doesn't mean he wants to be my labor coach."

"I'd be a good coach."

"I didn't say you wouldn't—"

"You two will do fine together."

Still keeping a low profile and his head down, Tommy edged his way around to the driver's side of the car.

"His shifts will probably conflict with the classes."

"I'll work out something," Danny said.

"I'll be sure his duty captain knows what's going on."

Stephanie glared at her father. What on earth had possessed the man to propose that Danny, of all people, become her childbirth coach? Didn't her father realize that meant Danny would be *touching* her? Intimately. Almost as intimately as if they were lovers.

Which they weren't. And weren't likely to be in this lifetime or any other.

The car's engine turned over, and Stephanie gasped, jumping about a foot in the air. Behind the windshield, Tommy grinned at her, his shyness suddenly vanished and replaced with the pride of accomplishment. The youngster was going to be a real charmer when his acne cleared up and he became a little more self-confident. Particularly, if in the meantime, he took lessons from Danny.

"Hey, I told you the kid was a genius," Danny said, grinning almost as foolishly as the boy.

"Sounds to me like everything is all arranged," her father said. "I'll get on home. I have to make some calls so there won't be any glitches while I'm gone."

The biggest glitch was thinking about Danny being present at the birth of her daughter. The mere thought was unsettling, as if he was the man who should have been there all along.

But she'd seen his near panic at her father's suggestion—or more accurately, her father's *command* to become Stephanie's childbirth coach.

That wasn't fair to Danny. Or to her. But she was damned if she knew what to do about it and hated that the possibility brought a secret thrill of longing that she'd be able to rely on Danny's strength if hers gave out.

THE PASEO DEL REAL SCHOOL district administrative offices were housed in a mission-style building with a red-tile roof located across the street from the high school. The cross-country team was running wind sprints around the football field and a couple of pickup basketball games were in progress on the asphalt courts.

Stephanie parked in a visitor slot, got out of her car and walked toward the main entrance. At a discount maternity clothing shop, she'd bought a semi-professional outfit for job hunting. The navy-blue blouse and skirt made her feel so dowdy she'd added a colorful scarf to loop around the collar and pinned it with a bright red heart. Knock-'em-dead-gorgeous, she wasn't, but it would have to do.

A clerk ushered her into the office of Ed Thornley, Director of Human Resources, according to the sign painted on his glass door.

He stood as she entered. "Ms. Gray, please have a seat." He gestured to the two straight-back chairs in front of his modest walnut desk.

"Thank you for seeing me."

"As you can imagine, the school district is always eager to cooperate with the city's fire chief."

Sitting down, she folded her hands demurely in her lap to prevent her fingers from trembling. She wished she could do something about her nervous stomach, too. "I didn't realize you would associate me with my father."

"I believe it was my secretary who recognized your name."

"I see." She hadn't thought to use her father's connections but at this point she'd welcome any edge she could get.

"Now, then." Mr. Thornley settled into his chair and tented his fingers under his chin. Her application was centered in the middle of his desk. "Tell me what type of job you're looking for."

"I've been teaching at a local preschool, and I love it, but my training is in art. I thought perhaps—"

"Oh, my dear, we only have two art teachers in the entire district, one at each high school, and neither of those fine ladies will be approaching retirement age anytime soon."

"Then perhaps you'd have an opening in the primary grades?"

"We may well have something in September, that's true. But if I'm reading your application correctly, you don't have a teaching credential."

"I do have a degree. With the teacher shortage—"

"There's no shortage in Paseo, my dear. Our district is considered prime territory with reasonable pay schedules and a stable student population. It's the inner city schools that have difficulty recruiting teaching staff."

Great, she'd have to move back to San Francisco in order to get a decent job, and that would put her in close proximity to Edgar Bresse. That wasn't an option she'd willingly consider.

"Now then, with your background we might consider you for a position as teacher aide. Of course, that's only part-time but since you're about to become a mother—"

"That's exactly why I need a full-time job. I need to be able to support myself and my baby."

"Ah." He nodded knowingly. "I'd really like to be of assistance, Ms. Gray, given your father's position in our fair city, but I'm afraid my hands are tied. Without a credential—"

"I understand, Mr. Thornley." She stood and extended her hand. "And I assure you, the fire department will continue to respond to any emergencies you might have even if you can't hire me."

"Yes, well, I didn't mean to imply otherwise."

"Of course not. Thank you for taking the time to meet with me."

She left his office discouraged but wiser. She hadn't planned to involve her father in her job search. She didn't think he'd approve. But obviously, that was a mistake. He knew virtually everyone in town. While he might not want her going to work, he was the best connection she had and she was darn well going to use him.

Station 6 where her father's office was located was on her route home.

HEFTING A COIL OF HOSE over his shoulder, Danny started up the stairs inside the training tower at Station 6. It was the crew's fourth trip through the exercise that afternoon, and his calves were beginning to burn, his shoulders ached, and sweat dampened the back and armpits of his motley gray workout shirt. But he was barely aware of any discomfort.

For the past three days, since Chief Gray had asked

him to fill in as Stephanie's labor coach, he'd been in a daze. A whirlpool had caught him, dragging him down, and he couldn't decide whether to fight against the pull or not.

It was one thing to be a friendly neighbor, making sure Stephanie got enough exercise and ate right. Watching out for her in a big brother sort of way. Even kissing her had its merits. Lots of them, he'd discovered.

If he went to the childbirth classes with her, that meant he'd be the one to coach her through labor. And *delivery*.

But helping her deliver her baby? That scared the hell out of him.

Granted, he'd had basic training about how to deliver a baby in an emergency but he'd never had to use the information and had hoped he never would. The film they'd shown was explicit—a screaming woman, her fear palpable on the screen, plenty of blood. The whole thing had made Danny sick to his stomach. He couldn't imagine watching Stephanie go through that kind of agony. No way.

He'd sooner walk through black smoke without a regulator.

Through the cut-out window at the third-floor landing, he spotted a movement down below, a flash of red, white and blue. *Stephanie!* Talking to one of the guys from Engine 61.

Without thinking, he dropped the coiled hose where he stood, grabbed the rappelling rope that dangled outside the window and slid to the ground.

Above him, someone yelled, "Sullivan! Get your butt back up here."

He ignored the order.

Instead, he played it cool, sauntering toward Stephanie as though he didn't have a care in the world. As though he hadn't just been thinking about her.

As though he didn't hope to hell she'd found someone else to be her childbirth coach.

"Hey, Twiggy, what's happening?"

Eyebrows raised, she looked him up and down like a movie critic who didn't enjoy the show. "I gather you've had enough training for today."

"Right. I'm in great shape. I'll let the other guys carry on without me while I fraternize with the civilians."

"Oh, they'll love that, particularly your duty captain."

"Yeah, he's a terrific guy." He looped his arm around her shoulders and walked her into the bay area where the trucks were parked, acing out the friendly chat Greg Wells was having with Stephanie. "Really nice of you to drop by to see me."

"You're so full of it, Sullivan. I came to see my father."

"Oh." His arm slipped from her shoulders. "I thought maybe—"

"I want him to help me find a job."

"You've already got a job. Besides, you're—"

"Pregnant. Not disabled. And sooner or later I'm going to have to support myself and move out of Dad's house."

"Why?" It seemed to him she had a pretty good deal going, a roof over her head, a caring father, close enough so Danny could keep an eye out for her. Not every unwed mother had it as good. Not that he'd deny her the right to a career if that's what she wanted but he couldn't understand the rush.

"Haven't you heard some women like to be independent?"

"Sure, but why now? Can't you wait till after the baby comes?"

Her eyelids fluttered closed, and he immediately missed seeing the golden sparks of rebellion that were so much a part of her personality.

"Maybe I'm feeling you and my dad and half the rest of the world are ganging up on me," she said quietly. "I'm losing control of my own life."

He cupped her chin, aware of the softness of her skin, the sweet, innocent scent of her perfume. Subtle yet enticing. "I'll back off anytime you say as long as I know you're going to be okay on your own." He swore he would, surprised at how deeply that possibility hurt.

"I'll hold you to that promise, Sullivan."

"Yeah, I know you will." If he hadn't been standing in the middle of the fire station with a couple of dozen guys hanging around, he would have kissed her. He was tempted to anyway. But he didn't think she'd appreciate the gesture. "So, do you want me to walk you to your dad's office?"

"He's not in. His secretary tells me he had a meeting at city hall."

"I could give you a tour of the place instead. Starting with my sleeping quarters, of course. We could test out the bed, see if it's wide enough for two."

"For *three,* in my case." Her lips curved with the hint of a smile. "Like you're going to seduce a woman who's nearly seven months pregnant into your bed?"

"Don't be so sure you're safe, Twigs. You're a very attractive package, no matter how pregnant you are." He gave her neck scarf a gentle tug. "Don't tempt me too much or I'll take you up on your offer."

"It wasn't an—"

"Yeah, I know. But a guy can dream, can't he?"

Her blush flamed as brightly as the red swirls on her scarf, and that tickled him. But somewhere in his gut, he wondered if he wasn't dancing on a high wire. It would take only a single misstep and he'd tumble to a place he'd never intended to go.

The jarring sound of the fire tone and Emma Jean's voice blaring over the loudspeaker gave him a punch of adrenaline.

"Engines 61 and 62, ladder company 66, rescue 6. Structure fire, corner of Sierra and Broadway. Multiple alarms."

Impulsively he leaned forward and brushed a kiss to Stephanie's cheek. "See you in the morning for our walk."

She blinked up at him, concern apparent in her eyes. "Be careful," she whispered.

"I always am." Turning, he jogged to Engine 62, stepped into his boots and pulled up his bunker pants, hooking the suspenders over his shoulders. Fighting a fire wasn't the only place he needed to be careful.

Grabbing his jacket, he swung up into the seat behind the driver and put on his helmet. A member of a firefighter's family, Stephanie understood the danger of a multiple-alarm fire as much as he did. And she was worried about him. He couldn't recall the last time a woman other than his mother had cared much one way or the other about what happened to him.

When it came to girlfriends, he'd intentionally played the field—superficial relationships, a few nights of fun, some laughs and then he'd split. The couple of times he'd come close to anything resembling permanence, he'd bailed out in a panic—like his father had—and found another woman to enjoy for a month or two. The women he dated had all known right up-front he wasn't in the game for the long haul. He'd never led them on about that.

So they hadn't worried about him when the engines rolled out of the fire station, sirens screaming.

He buckled his shoulder harness as the fire truck lurched forward. Stephanie was watching from the back of the bay out of harm's way. Watching him as though she cared.

He touched the brim of his helmet in a two-finger salute as the truck made the turn onto Paseo Boulevard, and he lost sight of her. But her image remained in his imagination. Straight and tall yet determined. Fiercely stubborn when she chose to be. A woman a man would like to have waiting for him when he got back from a fire.

A good reason to come home safe.

Chapter Seven

"You made the news last night."

"Not me. Dudley Do-Right handles the Public Information Officer gig."

Stephanie smiled as she walked beside Danny through the quiet residential area. Battalion Chief Dudley Dominic was all spit and polish, and the men weren't always supportive of his by-the-book rules. Neither was her father, for that matter. He believed in careful training and individual initiative; shiny shoes were at the bottom of the priority list for his men.

"Funny, I thought sure it was you posing by the ambulance trying to look heroic while they bandaged you up."

His hand went to the strip of white gauze on the back of his neck. "A falling brand got me. Occupational hazard. No big deal."

Maybe not for him but Stephanie's heart had lodged in her throat when she'd recognized him on the ten o'clock news and realized he'd been injured.

"Mother used to be terrified she'd see Dad on TV

on a stretcher, or worse, see his body covered by a sheet.''

"She didn't have to worry. They wouldn't release an injured firefighter's name until the next of kin was notified.''

"She knew that but it didn't help her sleep any better when Dad was working.'' They turned a corner to walk along a curving street lined with tidy lawns and flower beds and thirty-year-old tract homes that had gained some measure of individuality over time. As the population of Paseo had increased, new tracts had gobbled up the agricultural land on the outskirts of town, building two-story homes with three-car garages squeezed onto small lots. Stephanie preferred the older, more settled neighborhoods.

Danny had come by for their daily walk after his shift ended and before she had to leave for work at the preschool. Later he'd go for a run followed by a grueling bike ride, all part of his training regimen for the upcoming triathlon. The man had more energy than anyone had a right to have. Little wonder he didn't carry an extra ounce of fat on his body, only roped muscle and long, lanky sinew.

"Fighting fires isn't all that dangerous.''

"But terrible things can and do happen. Firefighters put themselves in harm's way.''

"Fortunately, the Paseo department's only lost one man since it was founded, which is bad enough, of course.''

"I know. Ray Gainer. Dad was desperately upset about that. He grieved as much as if he'd lost a son.''

"That's probably how he felt. Your dad's as loyal to his men as they come."

From what she'd seen, she suspected Danny valued his friendships, too, at least with his men friends. Women seemed to provide more transient relationships for him, here one moment and gone the next. Stephanie didn't want to fall into that latter category. She'd almost rather be one of his "buddies" and not risk her heart on a deeper attachment. The gamble wouldn't be worth it.

"I was a little surprised that Ray's widow married another firefighter so soon after his death," she commented, although not with disapproval.

"Right, Logan Strong, the best cook at Station 6 and a confirmed bachelor, or so we thought until he popped the question to Janice." His arms swung easily at his sides, his hands only inches from hers. "There was a rumor going around those wailing bagpipes he plays had finally damaged his brain."

"What an awful thing to say." She aimed her elbow for his ribs but he dodged out the way, circling a liquid amber tree at the curb that was bright with its new spring leaves.

"Yeah, I know." He grinned at her. "Just kidding."

"My mother warned us girls about marrying a firefighter. Can't believe Janice would do it twice, but then Logan is probably the exception to the rule."

"And I'm not?"

She eyed him with a haughty lift of her brows. "I suspect you're exactly the sort of man my mother was talking about." Which would be true whether he wore a firefighter's uniform or a business suit. He was simply too easy on the eyes, too much of a flirt, to be trusted with a woman's heart.

"Hey, I thought your parents were happy together."

"They were. It broke Dad's heart when she died of cancer. But that didn't mean my mother hadn't spent half her life worried about him."

"Ironic, isn't it, that your sister married a guy in Special Forces? That's got to be ten times more dangerous than fighting fires."

"Karen always was a bit of a rebel."

It was his turn to shoot his eyebrows up. "And you're not?"

Of course she was. Why else had she moved away from Paseo and sought a career and a little excitement in San Francisco? And look at the mess that had gotten her into. Maybe a few sleepless nights concerned about a husband's safety was a decent trade-off.

"Rebellion isn't all it's cracked up to be," she mumbled.

They walked to the next corner then turned onto their street. Stephanie checked her watch and broke into a jog toward home. "I've gotta dash or I won't get my shower before it's time for me to leave for school."

Danny matched her stride for stride. "Hey, no jogging. You'll jiggle the baby."

"The baby's fine. She likes a bumpy ride."

"If you say so." They reached her driveway, and

he slowed to a stop while she veered down the driveway toward the back door. "I'll pick you up about seven for the childbirth class."

She groaned. Maybe there would be a huge wildfire and all the off-duty firefighters would be called in to work. Which would leave Stephanie the only one in class without a partner.

She didn't know which thought was more demoralizing—being alone for something that should be a shared activity or having Danny touch her and not being able to touch him back.

THE HOSPITAL PARKING LOT was crammed with cars and a stream of visitors carried bouquets of flowers or stuffed animals toward the main entrance of the two-story structure.

As Danny whipped into a slot just vacated by an old pickup truck, he smiled, picturing himself bringing flowers for Stephanie and delivering a giant teddy bear for her baby. Or maybe he should get the kid a huge doll.

Hell, he didn't know what kind of present a baby would like. He'd never in his life bought anything for a female under the age of twenty, and then not often, he admitted. He didn't know squat about bottles or diapers. Hadn't particularly wanted to. He was the last person on earth who should go near a prenatal class.

He switched off the ignition and sighed.

"You don't have to do this, you know," Stephanie said. "I can wait till Dad's back home and start the next class."

"Not to worry. The firefighter's creed is to serve." He popped open his door, got out and hurried around to her side of the SUV, but she didn't wait for his help. Too darn independent for that. "You know where we're supposed to go?"

"The education wing. After we check in, they'll probably give us a tour of the maternity ward."

"Great." Instinctively he took her arm to usher her between the parked cars. The night air was cool, and she was wearing a bright yellow sweater in a soft nubby knit and dark slacks. He didn't touch her often but when he did, like now, an electric current hummed through his fingertips as though he'd grazed a live wire. She was one potent lady, although he didn't think she realized that was the case.

The automatic doors swished open for them and they entered the lobby. Upholstered chairs were scattered in conversational groupings between mock-marble columns. Two older women in pink volunteer jackets worked at an information booth in the center of the room. They smiled at Danny but Stephanie seemed to know where she was going, leading them down a corridor to the left.

"You've been here before?" Danny asked.

"More times than I care to remember—when mother was sick. They have support groups for cancer patients and their families."

Those couldn't be happy memories.

They made a turn into a new hallway, and Danny almost bumped into a nurse hurrying the opposite way.

"Hey, Addy," he said, immediately recognizing her from the various trips he or his fellow firefighters had made to the hospital. "What's happening, sweetheart? Are things so slow in the emergency room you have to round up your own patients?"

"Don't I wish, hon." She laughed warmly and glanced at Stephanie then back to Danny. "What brings you here?"

"Childbirth class."

Registering surprise, she dropped her gaze to Stephanie's midsection. "Well, congratulations. To both of you. I hadn't heard—"

"What did I tell you?" Stephanie said. She shrugged. "You explain it this time. I'm going to find the classroom."

"No, wait." He reached out to snare her arm but she was too quick for him.

"Oops, did I say something wrong?" Addy asked.

"No, everything's cool." He watched Stephanie striding down the hallway, her back as stiff as a pole. "I'm not the baby's father, though."

"Hmm, interesting." She got a curious twinkle in her eyes. "You're just filling in?"

"Something like that." Stephanie vanished through a door. "Look, I gotta go. Good to see you, Addy."

"Take care," she called after him.

He barely heard her, already at the door to the classroom. He scooted past the volunteer checking couples in at the desk and found Stephanie seated at a conference table toward the back of the room.

He slid into the molded-plastic chair beside her. "Why'd you take off so fast?"

"So you could be alone with your girlfriend while you explained—"

"She's not my girlfriend."

"No?" Stephanie cocked her brows. "You called her sweetheart."

"That doesn't mean anything. I call all the girls…well, that's not the point. She's the emergency room nurse on the swing shift. All the guys at the station know her. She's the one who stitches us together if we get banged up."

Stephanie's expression relented—marginally. "She called you hon."

"That's what she calls everyone, probably because she can't remember all our names."

"Are you saying you've never dated her?"

Unwilling to lie, he swallowed hard. Almost every man in the department had dated Addy at one point or another. She was a lot of fun to be with, almost one of the guys. But he'd never been serious about her. "A couple of beers, maybe. In a crowd. With the guys, you know? It was no big deal."

She humphed. "I wonder if that's how she felt about it. She certainly gave you an appreciative once over before she figured out I was pregnant."

"Aw, come on—"

"Good evening, moms-and-dads-to-be and coaches." A middle-aged woman in a floral-print medical jacket had taken center stage in front of the classroom. "I'm Maureen Truelove." She smiled in a self-effacing way. "Typecast from the day I was born, I'm afraid. Welcome to Paseo Community Hospital's expectant parent class."

"Look, Stephanie, I don't think you ought to—"

"Shh. I want to listen to this even if you don't." She shifted in her chair a quarter turn away from him, giving him the cold shoulder and a view of her aristocratic neck.

Damn! How did he get himself into this mess anyway? Sure, he owed Harlan Gray a lot. And he liked Stephanie more than he should. But he didn't *belong* here with her. Some other guy, the one she loved, should be sitting beside her. Caring about her. Concerned about her health, her well being and that of the baby they'd created together.

Danny knew darn well if she were carrying *his* baby no one could have kept him away from this class. Or Stephanie. No matter how scary the prospect of being a father might be.

Glancing around the room, he saw lots of telling body language going on. Couples holding hands. Leaning toward each other. Guys wrapping their arms around their woman's shoulders.

Meanwhile, he and Stephanie were like opposite poles of a magnet—resisting each other. How the hell would he be able to help her when it came time to deliver the baby if she didn't let him get close to her?

Despite the air-conditioned room, sweat began to creep down his spine. He didn't want to fail her.

"How long is the average labor?" one of the young women in the class asked as the class was touring the facilities.

"That varies so widely it's impossible to say," Maureen responded. She stood near the head of an ordinary-looking bed in the labor room talking to the eight couples that had squeezed into the room. The scent of antiseptic mixed with the sweeter perfume worn by one of the expectant mothers.

"My sister took twenty hours to deliver her first baby."

"For a first-time mother, that's not unusual. And remember some labors go much more quickly and some actually take longer. Either way, the delivery can be perfectly normal."

The group groaned in unison, not a woman in the class eager to consider a labor that went longer than twenty hours.

As the nurse continued to explain the process and the equipment available in the room, Stephanie became increasingly aware of Danny standing directly behind her. He was so close, she felt the heat of his body, the soft current of his breath warm across her neck. Other couples were standing with the husband's arms wrapped around his wife. A part of her—a feminine, needy part—wanted Danny to do the same.

Her good sense told her it would be better if he would step away. But there was nowhere for him to go. He was backed up against the couch where a husband or delivery coach could take a nap if the hours went on too long.

She couldn't move, either, not without shoving the couple who stood in front of her out of the way.

So she gritted her teeth and endured the unwelcome heat of desire curling through her midsection, trying not to imagine Danny making love to her.

"All right," Maureen said. "Let's step outside and turn to our right. We'll take a look at an actual delivery room, unless they're all occupied."

The delivery room looked more foreign than the labor room. More intimidating and *medical.*

With Danny practically joined at her hip now and making her so nervous, she wondered how she'd manage the greater intimacy of delivering a baby with him at her side. Of course, she wouldn't be thinking about having sex with him when the time came—a topic which seemed to be very much on her mind at the moment.

Still she couldn't imagine any situation that made a woman more vulnerable than giving birth. Danny would recognize her fear. See her weakness. She wouldn't be able to hide behind the screen of witty comebacks that she used to cover her real feelings.

Her only hope was to ask the doctor to knock her out early in the process so she wouldn't embarrass herself by crying and carrying on like a baby in front of Danny.

The tour finally led them to the nursery where the couples pressed their faces to the glass, oohing and aahing over the newborn babies.

At the sight of a set of twins snuggled together in

their shared bassinet, wrapped tightly in their blankets, emotion crowded into Stephanie's throat.

"Oh, Danny, look at the twins. Aren't they precious?"

"They're so small." The note of awe in his voice matched her own wonder.

"But everything's so perfect. Their tiny ears. Their little mouths." The emotion welled up, pressing tears to the back of her eyes. A silent sob shook her shoulders.

"Hey, Twigs, take it easy." As if he knew exactly what she wanted, he slid his arms around her middle and pulled her back against him, resting his cheek against her head. He cocooned her away from the other couples, whispering in her ear, "Your baby will be perfect, too."

"I know. They're just so beautiful and I'm...I'm so scared."

"Shh. You don't have to be. I'll be there with you every minute. I promise."

Trying to calm herself, to find some emotional distance, she drew a shuddering breath. "Maybe that's what I'm afraid of, that you'll be there laughing at me."

"Not a chance. I'll be too scared myself to give anyone a hard time. Hell, I'll be lucky if I don't pass out at the first sight of blood."

"You wouldn't," she gasped. That possibility was shocking. Danny was the most macho man she'd ever known. He'd never pass out like an ordinary mortal might.

"I could. Those darn training films they show of a woman giving birth in the back seat of a car always make me sick to my stomach. You watch, you'll be the one giving me smelling salts before this whole thing is over."

She almost laughed out loud. The image of her getting up from the delivery table to resurrect Danny after he'd fainted was so absurd it stretched credibility. And it was just what she'd needed to hear. He wasn't perfect, and he was scared, too.

"If you faint while I'm in the middle of labor," she chided him, "I'll never let you live it down."

"Great. Now you've turned this whole ordeal into a challenge, and you know I can't resist a challenge."

Turning her face, she brushed a kiss to his cheek. "Thanks."

"For what?"

"For making me feel like I'm not such a wimp." Looking into his bright blue eyes, she recognized it had been far too easy to fall in love with Danny and the most foolish thing she'd ever done in her life. It had happened while she wasn't looking. Blindsided her. And now, despite how unwise it might be, her loving Danny was a fait accompli. She couldn't turn back the clock.

Why couldn't a woman lead with her head instead of her heart?

MAKING IT THROUGH the firefighting academy didn't compare to the intensity of this ordeal, and things had just gotten worse.

The instructor had organized the couples with the men straddle-legged sitting behind their ladies, everybody on big, oversize pillows. Stephanie was cuddled up to Danny close enough for him to catch the scent of her shampoo. Violets, he thought, soft and sweet, as innocent as a spring day. But he wasn't feeling the least bit innocent at the moment.

"We're going to do a few relaxation exercises," Maureen announced, "and then we'll be done for this session. But don't forget to take along the handouts you received."

Danny wasn't sure he wanted to read any more about pregnancy and delivery. It was hard enough he'd had to confess he'd probably pass out at the critical moment. Some coach he was going to make.

"A woman experiences a lot of aches and pains during pregnancy," the nurse explained. "Her body is changing, muscles are stretching. Even her joints loosen as she prepares for delivery. Relaxation at every stage is critically important." She glanced around the room at her students. "And I'll give you a clue, gentlemen. Fifteen years from now when your wife is coping with an adolescent, these exercises will be even more welcome."

The couples tittered.

Danny didn't. It wasn't likely he'd be around Stephanie long enough to see her baby become a teenager.

The hell of it was that bothered him. More than it should.

"First, gentlemen, let's work on your partner's

neck muscles.'' Maureen strolled around the room, moving among the couples, smiling and offering encouragement. ''I want you to take your fingertips and massage from the top of her head down to her shoulders. Make your movements steady and firm as though you want to shove all that unwanted tension away. And, moms, I want you to close your eyes and think of something pleasant—a pretty sunset or a sailboat on the ocean. And breathe slowly.''

Danny did as instructed. In response, he heard Stephanie's soft moan of pleasure. Each time he did the exercise, her tension eased while his built to an uncomfortable level. He'd never touched her in this way, caressing her, measuring the silky texture of her hair, discovering the warmth of her flesh beneath his fingertips.

Following the teacher's directions, he moved his hands to her shoulders, kneading along her spine with his thumbs, aware that she was pliant and vulnerable to his touch. The ache that had begun hours ago grew more insistent behind the zipper of his jeans. A sheen of sweat dampened his forehead.

How long did the teacher expect him to keep this up without embarrassing both himself and Stephanie?

Stephanie's head lolled forward when Danny began massaging the small of her back. Her spine curved to an elegant arch, allowing him to explore the delicate shape of each vertebra with his fingertips, yet the thickness of her sweater frustrated his efforts. He wanted his hands on her. Skin to skin. All over her.

The teacher interrupted the exercise. ''All right,

moms. You've enjoyed yourself enough for the moment.''

At the sound of the teacher's voice, Stephanie started out of a pleasant haze of wanting. A chorus of protests went up from the women in the class but none more heartfelt than Stephanie's. She'd wanted the feel of Danny caressing her to go on forever.

''When is it our turn for a massage?'' one of the dads-to-be asked.

''Whenever you can talk your wife into it,'' Maureen responded with a laugh. ''One more thing and I'll let you go for tonight. How many itchy tummies do we have here?''

With a few embarrassed giggles, most of the pregnant women raised their hands, including Stephanie.

''Itchy?'' Danny mumbled.

''Sometimes it's awful,'' she admitted.

At the front of the class, Ms. Truelove produced a box of body lotion samples and began passing them out. ''Itching is normal, ladies. Your skin is stretching and trust me, the dry air we've been experiencing lately is making it worse. Try a daily dose of this moisturizer and see if it helps.''

''Can I get my husband to rub it on for me?'' a woman asked, a gleeful look in her eyes.

''I recommend it.''

Her cheeks still flushed with desire, Stephanie took the tube of lotion from the teacher and clutched it in her hand as tightly as a baton in a relay race. How could she get Danny to soothe the cream on her tummy, she wondered. Or did she really want him to?

Her skin was nearly on fire from his massage and so was her libido. No telling where things would lead if they were face-to-face with Danny caressing her as sweetly as he'd been massaging her neck and back.

Dear heaven! Who would have thought a man who hauled firehose around for a living would have such gentle hands?

With the class dismissed, the couples stood around visiting for a while. Stephanie could barely keep her mind on the conversation. She kept imagining Danny's hands on her belly...and on her breasts. And a good many other places she was afraid to picture in too much detail.

"So, are you ready to go?" she asked as casually as she could. "Tomorrow's a work day for both of us."

"Right." He extended his hand to one of the men who'd become his instant buddy. "See you next week, Harry. Take good care of Michele."

"I intend to," Harry replied, his arm looping casually around his wife's shoulders.

With a few more brief good-nights, Danny ushered Stephanie out of the classroom and into the hallway.

"How do you do that?" she asked.

As easily as if they had always been a *couple,* he took her hand and threaded his fingers through hers. "Do what?"

"Everybody's your friend after ten seconds. It takes me ages to warm up to strangers."

"You're shy?" He asked the question as though he'd never considered the possibility.

"Of course I am. All artists—well, maybe most—are a little introverted."

"Could have fooled me, Twigs. You sure as heck haven't ever been shy with me."

"I've known you all my life. That's different." It was also the crux of the problem. He no doubt still thought of her as the pesky kid down the street, and she was all too aware of the number of women who had passed through his life, none of whom had lingered long.

The hospital doors swished open for them and they stepped outside. The cool night air washed over Stephanie but didn't quite manage to put a chill on her overheated libido. The memory of Danny's caresses was still too fresh, the feel of his hand linked with hers too heated. His fingers were so hot, he had to have an overactive metabolism. A great man to curl up with on a cold winter night.

Except her own metabolism appeared to be working overtime at the moment.

He helped her into his truck, the back of his hand brushing the side of her breast as he took her arm. An accidental caress, she was sure, but no less erotic than if he'd intended it.

Chapter Eight

Overcome by a bad case of conflicting urges, Stephanie barely spoke on the way home. She fingered the tube of lotion, unscrewed the top and tightened it again. The plastic was slippery in her hands. Or maybe she was sweating.

She couldn't come right out and say, "Let's do what all the other couples are doing tonight. You rub this on my tummy and we'll see where it leads."

She'd never been that brazen with any man and certainly couldn't be with Danny. Besides, she was pregnant, which hardly qualified her as a potential seductress even if she did build up the nerve to suggest they test out the chemistry that was bubbling between them. At least it was boiling on her side of the truck.

How on earth would she survive the mortification if the swell of her belly repulsed him?

She should leave well enough alone. He hadn't asked to be her childbirthing coach. The job had been foisted on him by her father. And, despite that memorable kiss at the carnival, he hadn't volunteered to become her lover, either.

Nope, the better choice was for her to take a cold shower and curl up with the most boring book she could find so she wouldn't be tossing and turning all night wishing for things she shouldn't.

He pulled the SUV into her driveway and she started to get out on her own.

"I'll walk you in," he said.

"It's only twenty-five feet to the back door. I'm not likely to get lost."

"You forgot to leave any lights on and there's no one at home, right?"

"Dad left this morning for his seminar."

"Like I said—" He popped his door open and the overhead light flashed on. "I don't like the idea of you walking into a dark house alone."

Stephanie wondered, after all these years of alternately ignoring or teasing her, what in the world had possessed him to be a gentleman now when she wasn't feeling the least bit ladylike. Though she had enough female hormones raging through her system to open a pharmaceutical factory.

The street was quiet, the neighboring houses dark. The glow from the streetlights filtered through the trees at the curb, creating a lacy pattern of shadows and light on the lawn and driveway. The same theme repeated across Danny's tan windbreaker, skipping from one broad shoulder to another.

He reached the back stoop one step before she did, turned and held out his hand.

Inside her body, she felt a fine trembling begin. Wanting and need coalesced like two fast-flowing streams joining to form a river of desire. Her heart pumped hard, and a ringing began in her ears.

She placed the tube of lotion in his hand.

For a heartbeat, he was quiet, studying her with eyes so dark she could barely see them in the dim light.

"If the door's locked," he said in a low voice that barely broke the silence, "I think a key would work better."

"A key—" Flustered and mortally embarrassed, she dug into her pocket for her keys. "Sorry about that. I don't know what I was—"

"I'll do it." Taking the keys, he opened the door, reached inside and flicked on the kitchen light.

She ducked her head to hide her face. "Well, good night. Thanks for coming to the class with me." She scooted past him, but to her surprise he followed her into the kitchen.

"You may need these again sometime." He held out her keys.

"Oh, right." She took them and dropped them into her pocket without looking at him.

"How's the itchy tummy?"

"Huh, fine. You know, there's always a little—"

"You want to see if this cream stuff works?"

Her head snapped up. She saw the same look in his eyes she'd seen the night he'd kissed her—sexy and heated without a hint of teasing. She swallowed hard.

"I'll try some when I get ready for bed."

If it were possible, his eyes grew even darker. "I got the feeling from Maureen that it worked best when applied by a partner."

Despite the fact that her heart was racing and her lungs were screaming for oxygen, she could barely draw a breath. "You don't have to."

"Part of the job training to be a coach." He hesitated, his gaze sweeping over her flushed face. "Unless you don't want me to."

"I'm fat."

"You're pregnant. Having a bulge around the middle comes with the territory." He skimmed the back of his fingers across her cheek. "You're also beautiful."

Tears flooded her eyes. "Danny, I—"

"Shh. We'll try some of the cream. If you don't like it, if I make you uncomfortable in any way, I'll stop. I promise."

Unable to speak, she managed to nod.

He led her into the living room, turned the end-table lamp on low and sat her down on the couch. Then he lowered himself beside her and opened the tube of lotion. He rubbed some of the cream between his fingers.

"Smells like roses," he said, a half smile curling his lips. "You ready?"

Every part of her being cried out for the first touch of his hand on her. "Yes," she whispered.

He slipped his hand beneath her sweater. His fingertips grazed over her flesh, soothing and sensual, his caress as sweet as a summer breeze and intimately arousing. She swallowed a whimper of pleasure.

"You have the softest skin," he murmured, holding her gaze with his. "And you make the nicest noises."

"You have great hands."

"Does that mean the cream's working?"

"I can't tell." She was experiencing too many sensations to sort them out. The masculine roughness of his hands. The elusive scent of roses mixing with his warm breath. The growing ache that was pulsing between her legs.

"Then we'll have to keep trying, won't we?" He squeezed some more lotion onto his fingertips then slipped them beneath the stretchy waistband of her slacks and under the sheer fabric of her panties.

"Oh," she moaned.

"Nice?"

"Very."

He skimmed back and forth, his fingers slipping lower with each trip across her belly. Each slow pass sent new ripples of pleasure through her like the wings of a butterfly. But hotter as though the wings carried tiny sparks of fire on their tips.

"Stephanie, honey, this might go better if I could see you. Would you mind if I lifted your sweater?"

She breathed out a sigh. "No."

"No, you don't mind? Or no, you don't want me to?"

"Yes, I want you to." Heedless of her fears, she

tugged her sweater up over her head with trembling fingers and tossed it aside.

For a moment, she thought she'd made a dreadful mistake. He stared at her, unmoving, his thoughts unreadable.

A feeling of shame crept behind her sternum and pressed painfully against her heart. He hated what she looked like. Hated that she was fat with another man's child.

To her amazement, he knelt in front of her and cupped the sides of her belly with his hands. His expression shifted and softened to one of reverence.

"No one ever told me how truly beautiful a pregnant woman could be. It never occurred to me that you—" Lowering his head, he pressed a soft kiss to her belly button. "You are so incredible."

In relief, she threaded her fingers through the thick waves of his hair. "I used to have an innie, now it's an outie."

He chuckled, a low rumbling sound that vibrated against her skin. His tongue circled her belly button, and her insides clinched.

"Danny?"

"Hmm, delicious." He lifted his head and his hands moved upward. Expertly his fingers unhooked her bra, and he took the weight of her breasts into his palms. "Whatever did you do with my Twiggy?"

"I was never *your* Twiggy. I was the pesky kid down the street."

"You're grown up now."

Grown and knowing exactly what she wanted.

"Kiss me, Danny. Kiss me like you did at the carnival." She hooked her hand around his neck, drawing him to her.

There was no hesitation on his part. With a hungry sound, his mouth covered hers and his tongue plunged inside. She was swept away by his need, which she fully matched with her own. He was her adolescent dream come true, her fantasy in the flesh, kissing her with a passion she never could have imagined in her teenage years. Even now it seemed surreal that she was kissing Danny Sullivan in her living room and hoping he would never stop.

He pressed her down on the couch, his hands fondling her breasts, his lips pressing kisses to them. When he took her nipple in his mouth, suckling, she cried out in unadulterated joy.

Her flesh had never been more sensitive, her body never more responsive than at this very moment with this man. She celebrated that realization.

"Stephanie, honey." He was breathing hard. The sure evidence of his arousal pressed against her thigh. "I don't know how far to go here, sweetheart. I don't even know if you can—"

"All the way, Danny. In every way you can."

"I don't want to hurt you."

She palmed his cheek, feeling the slight rasp of his evening whiskers. "You won't. Not unless you stop now." Tomorrow might be a different matter, she knew. But for tonight she was ready to risk anything to live out her dream of loving Danny Sullivan, the bad boy from down the street.

"The bedroom?" he asked.

She reached for the snap on his jeans. "I don't think I can wait that long."

She didn't have to. They made short work of the clothes they were wearing, tossing shoes and pants aside, before Danny stretched out beside her on the couch. His hand covered her belly and he started kissing her again. Soon his fingers dipped lower.

She couldn't help herself. At the first touch of his fingertip, she cried out his name. Lights exploded behind her eyes, blues and reds combining in a brilliant shade of violet.

"Oh, my," she sighed as she regained her breath.

"You're so responsive."

"It's the pregnancy. Lots of hormones."

"No. I think it's who you are."

"Your turn," she whispered.

"We'll do it together." He spread her legs. "You tell me if anything hurts. I won't want to stop but I swear, no matter when, I will."

"Over my dead body." She lifted her hips to meet him more than halfway. Yet, despite her readiness, she found him larger than she expected. It took a moment for her to accommodate him, and he waited so sweetly, so patiently, she could have cried at the sacrifice she knew he was making.

"You okay?" he asked. A muscle pulsed in his jaw and his neck was corded in self-restraint.

"Not yet, but I'm about to be." She hooked her legs around his waist and welcomed him into her body.

At first she noted the care he took with her, the incredible limitations he placed on himself. But even that was so arousing she lost herself in the sense of him filling her. Completing her in a way she'd never before experienced.

There was no passage of time. Only the sound of their breathing, the rhythmic movements of their bodies, their matching cries of release followed by the silence in the room.

Outside a car passed by, its headlights sweeping across the front windows. In the far distance, a siren sounded, an ambulance or fire truck, she couldn't be sure which. She only knew that somehow the arms that held her now were the only arms she'd ever want to feel holding her again.

DANNY'S ARM MUSCLES SHOOK with the effort to keep the bulk of his weight off of Stephanie. He'd tried to be so careful of her, tried not to hurt her, yet he'd never experienced lovemaking that was quite so potent. She'd taken every bit of what he had to offer and asked for more.

Her generosity awed him. Her passion inflamed him. She was more of a woman than any he'd ever known.

Together, they'd been so hot, they'd come close to spontaneous combustion.

Easing away, he stretched out beside her on the now too-narrow couch and held her. That they hadn't even made the effort to get to a bedroom spoke volumes about how aroused they had both been.

My God, if someone had asked him even a few months ago if he'd ever make love to Stephanie—much less on the living-room couch with her dad out of town—he would have laughed in their face. She was the kid from down the street. The boss's daughter. A woman who deserved commitment.

Now he couldn't imagine *not* making love with her.

But nothing had changed. She was still a woman who needed and deserved more than he could give.

Brushing a kiss to her forehead, he sat up and reached for his briefs. "That was a heck of an encore to the birthing class, Twigs. Maybe they ought to check the curriculum."

"You don't approve?" She struggled to a sitting position and he handed her her bra. Her nubby sweater had ended up stuffed between a cushion and the back of the couch.

"I'm already looking forward to next week." And wondering how in hell he'd keep his hands off Stephanie until then *and* avoid a repeat of this evening's activities after the class. If her dad knew what he had done, Harlan Gray would probably put his head on a spike and march it around the station house as a warning to any other guy who might get ideas about his daughter.

He tugged on his jeans and slipped his feet into his low-cut boots, not bothering to lace them.

"I better move my truck so the neighbors don't start talking."

"There's no rush. I could fix you some coffee. Or a drink?"

Standing, he looked down at her, her mussed hair and pale cheeks. Her stark expression of vulnerability. And he cursed himself. He never should have let things go this far.

"This wasn't a good idea, was it?" she said softly.

"You were terrific. Honest, Stephanie, I've never known another woman who—"

"But you're having morning-after regrets and it isn't even midnight yet."

Sitting on the edge of the coffee table, he finger-combed her hair, straightening the wayward strands. "I think we both kind of got carried away."

She gave him a tremulous smile. "Who would have thought a pregnant woman like me could seduce a guy like you?"

"Funny, I thought I was the one who seduced you." Taking her hand in his, he placed a kiss in her palm. "I can't give you what you need, Stephanie."

"You were doing a pretty good job a few minutes ago."

"I'm not good at commitment."

She withdrew her hand and glanced away but not before he saw tears glistening in her eyes. "Apparently I have a penchant for attracting men like that."

"This Edgar guy of yours is a slug not wanting to marry you the minute he knew you were pregnant. He could still come knocking on your door."

Her quick laugh didn't ring true. "Not much chance of that. Edgar Jared Bresse the Third doesn't often change his mind."

"The *third?*"

"Hmm, old San Francisco money. Very snooty."

"That probably means the first Edgar was nothing more than a lucky gold miner."

Standing, she stepped away, turning her back to him as she pulled on her slacks. "Actually they made their first killing by selling picks and shovels to the miners. Then they bought up half of downtown San Francisco after the earthquake and fire."

"Opportunists."

"Smart business people. Going into advertising made Edgar a bit of a black sheep as far as his parents were concerned, particularly since he's their only son." She straightened her sweater and gave her hair a toss, then turned back to Danny looking more composed than she had moments ago. Gutsy lady.

"Seems like if Edgar won't take financial responsibility for the baby, maybe his parents would—"

"I don't need or want their money. And frankly, Mrs. Bresse is such a cold, hard woman, I'm not sure I want my baby anywhere near her."

Gutsy *and* independent. Pretty darn stubborn, too. All of which were admirable qualities but none more so than her potent sexuality. Which Danny vowed to keep at arm's length from now on—or die trying.

He shifted uneasily. "Guess I'd better be going."

"If I can't talk you into coffee…"

She left the thought dangling, giving him the choice to stay or leave. That wasn't any choice at all. He was so far in over his head, he was at the bottom of an elevator shaft with no way to get back up.

"It's getting late."

She shrugged.

"I'll come by in the morning before I—"

"No, don't. I, uh, have to be at school early tomorrow."

"If you're sure."

Folding her arms over her stomach as a shield against the emotions that were raging through her, Stephanie nodded and prayed she wouldn't burst into tears. She didn't want Danny to know how badly he'd hurt her. Didn't want to admit, even to herself, what a fool she'd been.

"I'm sure." That she could get the words past the lump in her throat amazed her.

She waited in the living room while he left. She heard the back door open and close. A moment later the truck started, the headlights came on and swept past the window as he drove away.

Only then did she allow the lump in her throat to form tears, which ran down her cheeks.

Chapter Nine

Danny stroked his arms one after the other through the chilly ocean water. The two-and-a-half-mile swim was the hardest part of the triathlon for him, the most difficult part of his training regimen. Without much body fat, he had little natural buoyancy and sank below the surface between every stroke.

Today he welcomed the bitter taste of salt in his mouth, the burning sensation in his eyes and in his lungs, the ache in his arms and legs.

He hadn't seen Stephanie in three days. He'd been punishing himself ever since the night they'd made love, and he damn well deserved this kind of torture.

How could he have been so stupid?

How could he have hurt her so badly?

He staggered out of the water and dropped down on the sand. On race day he'd be looking at an endless bike ride after the swim and then a run on top of that, all in memory and celebration of the lives of the buddies he'd lost in Idaho. But for the moment he could rest.

He looked back toward the line of waves rolling

toward the shore. Tommy appeared on a crest then dipped out of sight. The kid was doing fine, getting stronger every day, although it was fortunate the junior division race involved shorter distances. But damn, the kid was determined.

In his own way as stubborn as Stephanie.

A cool breeze washed over Danny, raising gooseflesh, and he grabbed his towel, wrapping it around his shoulders while he waited for Tommy to reach the shore. Within minutes the boy stumbled up onto the beach.

Danny checked his watch. "Good job, kid. You took ten seconds off your time."

The boy gulped in great lungs full of air. "A personal best?"

"You got it." He grinned at the youngster. "So have you told Rachel what you're up to?"

"Naw. I'm afraid I might drown or fall off my bike, or something. I'll tell her after."

"No, no. You gotta tell her now, casual like. She'll be impressed that you're entering the race at all, and then if you mess up—" He shrugged. "She'll be sympathetic."

"You think?"

"Trust me, when it comes to the ladies, I'm an expert."

That was a damn lie. At least when it came to Stephanie, he didn't know what to do. Or even how to act, now that he'd crossed that invisible line between friends and lovers.

In comparison, the other women he'd known had

been easy. He could love 'em and leave 'em, walk away without either him or the woman getting hurt. They both knew the rules. With a couple of small exceptions—which had proved the point he was incapable of commitment—it had all seemed so simple.

Simple didn't begin to explain how he felt about Stephanie. Confused was far closer to the truth.

He'd promised to be her birthing coach. He couldn't renege on that. She needed someone to be there with her. Her boyfriend had let her down. Danny refused to leave her in the lurch, too.

But he wasn't sure she'd want him around after his disappearing act the other night.

Nor was he sure he could be close to her without wanting to make love with her again.

"You got a problem, coach?" Tommy asked. He scrubbed at his spiky hair with a towel, then wrapped it around his shoulders, shivering.

"Yeah, I do." Danny got to his feet. His job was to be Tommy's coach *and* Stephanie's. He was damn well going to do the best job he could in both cases. "Come on, kid. Ten miles on our bikes before we slack off for the afternoon."

Tommy groaned but struggled upright. "Maybe I'll get a chance to say something to Rachel in math class next week."

"Good plan, kid. A triathlon will wow her, I promise." He could only hope he'd find something equally impressive in order to get back on Stephanie's good side without risking a repeat of their heated night together.

STEPHANIE WAS GRATEFUL to have a Saturday to herself. She'd done the grocery shopping, changed sheets on her bed and her father's, and managed three loads of wash. She'd intended to take a nap but to her dismay she'd found herself looking out the damn kitchen window trying to spy on Danny, and she'd never lain down.

When in heaven's name would she learn?

He had no interest in her for a permanent relationship. He was right. She—and her baby—needed a permanent commitment or they would be better off alone.

He wasn't into commitment.

And she hated the thought that she'd always be alone.

With a yank, she opened the refrigerator and stared inside. You'd think after spending a small fortune at the grocery store there'd be *something* worth eating in the house. She really should have called a friend to go out. Except most of her girlfriends were married now and had children of their own. Or they'd moved away.

She'd have to start over making a whole new set of friends. Maybe the YWCA had a single-moms' club.

Leaning her head against the refrigerator, she sighed. No sense to feel sorry for—

An odd noise interrupted her thoughts. Someone was outside. In her backyard.

More curious than fearful, she went out the kitchen door and walked alongside the house toward the backyard. The faint smell of burning charcoal scented the air.

She turned the corner and her heart did a stutter step at the sight of Danny fussing over her dad's portable barbecue on the patio.

"Don't you have a barbecue at your place?" she asked, trying to keep her unwelcome surge of excitement at bay.

Glancing up, he shot her a quick grin. "I thought this would be easier."

"And why is that?"

"Since we're going to eat the steaks here, it didn't make any sense to cook them at my place then let them cool off getting them here."

"You're making me dinner," she concluded cautiously.

"Yeah, I figured with your dad gone you might not be eating regular meals. You know, just eating snacks and stuff." He poked at the glowing briquettes with the tongs.

"I did a huge grocery shopping today." Which somehow resulted in having nothing in the house to tempt her waning appetite. A problem she no longer had according to her loudly growling stomach.

"You can save whatever you bought for another night. These steaks are too good to pass up." At the picnic table on the covered patio, he unwrapped two beautiful T-bones. There was a big bowl of salad on the table and what she guessed was a loaf of garlic bread wrapped in foil. "And wait till you see what I brought for dessert."

"I gather you've decided to fatten me up?" More likely, this was his way of apologizing. But she didn't know if he was sorry he'd made love to her or regretted he wasn't interested in a commitment.

From the end of the picnic table, he picked up an oversize paperback book and flipped through the pages. "According to this, a well-rounded diet including all the food groups is important during pregnancy. It helps the baby develop normally."

"You bought a book on pregnancy?"

"And what to expect during delivery. I thought Maureen might forget something in the class or we'd have questions between sessions. This book seems to cover about everything under the sun. I figured we both ought to be prepared for anything that could happen."

Stunned by his thoughtfulness and equally confused by his touching gesture, she took the book from him. "I thought you'd want to bail out of being my coach."

"Heck, no. Once I make a promise, I'm in it for the long haul."

Instinctively she rested her free hand on her belly. Her baby needed a man like that. So did she.

Unwilling to let him see the tears of gratitude that flooded her eyes, she sat down at the table and glanced through the book, checking the topic headings. Fetal movements. Packing for the hospital. Breastfeeding. Having sex.

"It says the baby doesn't know we had sex."

Danny choked, coughed, and the barbecue tongs

clattered to the concrete patio floor. "God, I never even thought about—"

She stifled a laugh at the look of abject horror on his face. "You're safe. I don't think she'd come after you with a shotgun anyway."

"That's not what I meant."

"I know. Let's just forget about what happened the other night, okay?" As if she could, she thought, trying to ignore the ache in her chest. But if she couldn't have Danny as a lover, she needed him as a friend. That was far more important. "I'll go back to being the pesky kid down the street, and you can go on being my exasperating neighbor."

"Who makes you dinner."

"That's obviously the best kind of exasperating neighbor, if you're stuck having one."

"Yeah, right." His wry smile eased her wounded heart, if only a little. "You're okay, Twigs. If it means anything to you, I still think Edgar was a fool to let you walk away."

She shrugged. "I'm glad he showed his colors now instead of having to deal with a divorce later."

"I suspect my mother would have agreed with you. The worst part for her was my father simply turning his back on his family and walking away."

"That had to hurt." Both Danny and his mother had been wounded by his father's desertion. In Danny's case, the scar was invisible but Stephanie sensed it was still there.

"How's your mother doing now?" She recalled hearing Danny's mother had married the produce man at the local grocery store a few years ago. Evidently the romance bloomed between the artichokes and zucchini shortly before her groom's retirement.

"Great. Apparently she and Jake love being on the road in his RV. It's been like a three-year honeymoon for her. They're talking about finally settling down in Arizona."

"She deserves all the happiness she can get."

Danny nodded his agreement. "She's going to give me the house, sort of a belated wedding present in reverse."

"That's very nice of her."

"Yeah, it is." He fussed with the charcoal, making sparks fly. "The house needs some work, though. I've been thinking maybe you'd help me out redecorating the place."

"I'd be happy to." The possibility filled her with excitement along with the troubling thought that someday another woman might reap the benefits of whatever talents she contributed toward renovating Danny's house.

"That'd be great. Thanks."

The steaks began to sizzle on the barbecue, smoke billowing, scenting the entire backyard with the smell of charcoal and meat cooking.

Stephanie made a show of studying the book while Danny went about the business of setting the table and adding dressing to the salad. But she was acutely aware of him moving around the patio, looking very much as if he belonged there. His khaki walking shorts revealed well-muscled legs lightly furred with dark hair; his T-shirt displayed his broad shoulders tapering to a narrow waist.

She recalled every inch of his body, the hard plains and valleys created by hours of working out, all in contrast to the gentle way he had loved her. Despite what she'd told him, she'd savor those memories for the rest of her life. There'd be no forgetting for her.

He served their plates and sat down opposite her at the table. "Here you go, steaks a la Sullivan."

Tasting her first bite, she relished the succulent flavor. "You missed your calling. You should have been a chef instead of a firefighter."

"Oh, I get plenty of chances to cook at the station, assuming Logan doesn't feel like doing one of his specialties. But we don't often have steak. Too expensive for our budget."

Stephanie ate in silence for a few minutes, unable to shake the sensation of electricity in the warm evening air. The same sort of potent force that had drawn them together the night of the childbirth class, which Danny was now determined to ignore. So be it, she told herself. But that was a lie, too. She'd leap right into his arms if he'd so much as crook his little finger at her.

Foolish woman.

"So how's it going at the preschool?" he asked between bites.

"Fine, except the woman I'm replacing will be ready to come back to work about the time my baby is due, and Alice can only afford one teacher's aide."

"Does that mean you've been out job hunting?"

"If you call batting my head against the wall job hunting, yes."

"That bad, huh?"

"I went to a temporary agency yesterday. All the guy was interested in was my typing speed and how many different kinds of word processing programs I know. The fact that I have a college degree didn't mean squat to him, particularly since it's in art. I'm not exactly big-time employable."

"Something will turn up."

"I suppose. I asked Dad to keep an eye out for me but he's being very chauvinistic about me leaving the baby with a sitter or in day care too soon. He says I don't need to work as long as I'm living here."

Danny chewed thoughtfully for a moment, then said, "Why don't you open your own advertising company? You could work right out of the house until you built up your business. That way you wouldn't be leaving the baby."

"Paseo isn't exactly a mecca for advertising firms."

"But somebody is placing ads in the newspaper. And I see local ads on the TV all the time, most of which stink. You could do better, couldn't you?"

Yes, she could, now that she thought about it. But starting her own business would be risky, though not any more so than remaining unemployed, or worse yet, working at a local hamburger stand.

"I don't know," she said. "I'm basically a stranger to the market here, and I'd have to invest quite a bit of money for start-up costs." Mentally she ticked off the equipment she'd need. A computer capable of doing graphic art and a color printer. For video work, she could rent the equipment or hire freelancers. Her old drawing board was stuffed in her closet.

"Your dad would help you out, I'm sure. So would I, if it came to that." He leaned forward, pointing the business end of his fork at her. "You know, you ought to talk to Kim Lydell, Jay's wife. She's with the university now but she used to work at KPRX-TV. I bet she'd know something about the local market and who's handling the advertising business around here. It would be worth a shot, anyway."

Stephanie considered the possibilities. It wouldn't cost her anything to talk with Kim. She didn't really think it would lead anywhere but what the heck. She could at least give it a try. Kim was part of the fire-fighter family now and would help if she could.

"All right, I'll call her." Although she'd eaten only half her steak, Stephanie shoved her plate aside. "I'm stuffed."

"We're not done yet." Reaching down beside the table, he produced a blender and set it on the table.

She shook her head in amazement. How he'd dragged all the food and supplies from his house to hers without her noticing was a mystery to Stephanie.

He held up a bunch of bananas. "The *pièce de résistance*—a banana milk shake."

"Danny, I couldn't. You're going to turn me into a blimp."

"Not a chance, Twigs. Besides, I got this recipe

out of that pregnancy book. It's guaranteed to be low fat.''

She laughed. She couldn't help herself. Danny was the most endearing, the most maddening man she'd ever known. If he was planning to be this attentive clear up to her delivery date, how on earth could she possibly protect her heart?

As if she hadn't lost it to him years ago and had only just now recognized how foolhardy that had been.

Not wanting him to read her emotions, she said the first thing that popped into her mind. ''I thought I'd do some shopping for the baby tomorrow. You know, look at cribs, diaper pails, the basics I'll need.''

He paled and swallowed visibly. ''Sounds good. I've got the day off. How 'bout I tag along?''

''You don't have to,'' she said, surprised he'd even consider shopping with her. ''I'll be fine on my own.''

''Oh, no, you don't. You're not going to get rid of me that easily. Besides, given your delicate condition, you're going to need someone to carry all the stuff you buy.''

Reaching across the table, she took his hand. ''It would be nice not to have to shop alone but it's above and beyond the call of duty for a birthing coach. Like most men, you probably hate shopping anyway.''

He glanced at their hands, his far larger and a shade or two darker than hers. His thumb skimmed over her knuckles, sending a flurry of gooseflesh up her arm.

''Hey, my mom taught me power shopping from

an early age. We'll be in and out in an hour,'' he promised.

HE'D MADE IT HOME SAFELY.

Not once had he leaned forward to kiss Stephanie just for the pleasure of tasting her again. Though he'd been sorely tested more than once, tempted to lick a bit of steak sauce from the corner of her lips. Or kiss away the mustache left there by the foamy milk shake.

By sheer force of will, he'd managed *not* to carry her into the house and make love to her on the kitchen table, knowing full well he wouldn't have made it as far as the living room this time.

Yep, eating outside on the patio had been a stroke of genius.

Maybe the neighbors hadn't been watching but the fact they might be had kept him at arm's length.

Arm's length and sweating nails, he thought with a grimace as he dropped the leftover dinner fixings onto his own kitchen table. He'd nearly lost it altogether when she'd held his hand. So sweet. So seductive. As hard to resist as going into a smoke-filled room without an air pack when you knew someone needed rescuing.

How many weeks was it until the baby was due? The baby he was beginning to think of in far more personal terms than simply *Stephanie's* baby—a baby that meant something important to *him,* too.

And how the hell was he going to survive however long their time together would be without making love to Stephanie again? At this point, *he* was the one who needed rescuing from his overactive libido.

He glanced at the stove clock. It was too early to go to bed. And there wasn't enough cold water in the entire county for the number of showers he'd need to cool his simmering lust so he could sleep.

He'd have to go for a run. A long one.

"YOU'RE NOT GOING TO MAKE HER sleep in that pink frilly thing, are you?" Danny was scowling at a white crib lined with Little Bo Peep bumper pads edged with lace, the mattress covered by a matching sheet.

"I am having a girl, you know."

"Yeah, but this looks so frou-frou. The fire engines would be better." He pointed out an adjacent crib in a walnut finish.

"Fire engines are for little boys."

"Better not let your dad hear you being so sexist. Definitely not politically correct in Paseo. Girls can grow up and become firefighters if they want to. We've got a couple in the department and they do just fine on the job."

"You're impossible, Sullivan. I'm not going to have my little girl staring at fire engines all day." Shaking her head, she checked the price tag on the white crib. This was supposed to be a discount store but from the looks of things, she'd be better off checking out the weekly throwaway newspaper for a good, used crib.

"Didn't you want to be a firefighter when you were

growing up?'' He set a fire engine mobile in motion over the crib.

''Not me. Briefly I considered being the first female professional baseball player. You know, sort of a Jacqueline Robinson. But I changed my mind after I got hit in the head with the ball.''

''Ah, that explains everything.''

She threw a jab at his arm and missed when he jumped out of the way.

''What do you think about teddy bears?'' she asked as she moved to the next display crib. ''I'm going to put the baby in my sister's old room but I don't want to redecorate too much because I don't plan to stay at Dad's house any longer than I have to.''

Coming up beside her, he fingered the baby-blue bumper pad printed with dancing pink and green teddy bears. ''You're determined to be independent, aren't you?''

''I'm hardly in a position to rely on anyone except myself.''

''Yeah, and that stinks, too.''

''It's not exactly what I had intended to happen when the time came for me to have a baby,'' she admitted.

''If anyone can handle it, you can.''

She glanced up at him and got an odd sense of pride at the sincerity in his eyes. He wasn't teasing her. He really did think she could make it on her own.

''Thanks,'' she said.

He shrugged in response and edged away from her

as though he'd come too close, had revealed too much.

She understood he'd only agreed to hang in there as her coach—and her friend—until the baby arrived. Then he, too, would walk away. She wished that thought didn't hurt so much.

"So what about the teddy bears?" she asked.

"They're generic enough so you could use the same gear for your next kid."

She sputtered a laugh. "I'd certainly have to rely on someone else for that kind of a miracle."

"You'll find someone, Twigs. Edgar's not the only fish in the sea."

"But you're not volunteering to get caught in my net, huh?"

A stain of red colored his cheeks. "So are you going to buy the teddy bears?"

"Not yet. I need to think about it first." Turning away, she walked toward the back of the store. "I want to look at car seats now."

Danny checked his watch. What the hell! They'd been in this same store for almost two hours. He could have furnished an entire house in this much time. So much for his bragging about power shopping.

Stephanie dawdled over everything. Cribs. Changing tables. Dressers. Diaper bags. Infant swings. And now car seats. This whole ordeal was endless, and with each passing moment he felt like he wanted to be more than an observer. He wanted a real say in teddy bears vs. prissy ballerinas.

If Stephanie were carrying *his* daughter, his vote would count. But he didn't have the right.

He caught up with her. "I thought I came along to carry stuff for you. So far you haven't bought a thing."

Hauling a car seat off the shelf, she placed it in the middle of the aisle to examine it more carefully. "You must have misunderstood. I said *shopping,* not buying. I need to check out what's available before I make any decisions."

He gave a strangled groan. They could be at this for days!

"Have you considered taking one of the store's catalogs home and making your decisions there?"

"It's better when I can actually touch things. But if you're bored—"

"Okay, here's another idea," he said, a little desperately now. "Let's make some tentative decisions, like the teddy bears. We'll schlep the stuff back to your house, set it up and take a look. If you don't like it, we'll bring it back. How's that?"

"What if I find the same thing later at a lower price? I can't afford to—"

"I can. We'll put everything on my Visa. Worst case, I have to bring stuff back and they give me a credit." He hooked his arm through hers, which was a mistake because she felt so good to touch. "Come on. I'll show you power shopping made easy."

"You're being bossy again."

"Nope. I'm saving you from yourself. At the rate you're going, the kid will be two years old and too big for a crib before you make up your mind. And she'll be twisted because she's been sleeping on the floor the whole time.''

Stephanie protested again, though not too forcefully. So he found a clerk—which was no easy trick—and put their shopping trip into high gear. Crib. Teddy bear sheets and bumper pads plus a matching quilt, which she objected to as being too expensive. A musical mobile along the same theme. A white changing table that matched the crib.

Finally Stephanie dug in her heels, insisting they'd spent enough for one day.

Danny relented, except as they headed for the cash register a display of soft, cuddly teddy bears caught his eye. He picked up one and handed it to Stephanie.

''This will look good in the crib.''

She hugged it to her chest, rubbing her cheek across the top of its head. ''I'm going to pay you back for all of this.''

''Not for that teddy bear, you won't. It's a special gift from me to her.'' He brushed his hand gently over her stomach.

She nodded and mouthed the words, ''Thank you.''

He figured her emotions were on edge and she couldn't speak. He was getting a little choked up about the whole thing, too. But a macho guy like him couldn't let on.

TWO HOURS LATER, Danny had a three-sided crib upside down in what would be the baby's room, giving new meaning to the phrase, ''Some assembly required.'' The room was littered with packing material and cardboard boxes. The one thing that appeared to be missing were the instructions to put the damn crib together.

''I'm telling you, we're missing a set of screws for this side of the crib,'' he said.

''I'll look around Dad's workbench in the garage. Maybe he's got something that will work.''

Sitting back on his haunches, he splayed his fingers through his hair. In about two minutes he was going to make an emergency call to Tommy Tonka. Maybe the kid could make sense of this jigsaw puzzle.

Stephanie returned with an assortment of nuts, bolts and screws in her hand. ''Try these.''

She looked as fresh as when they'd started the shopping trip, her hair neatly combed, her floral blouse dazzling bright. In contrast, Danny felt like he'd been run over by a couple of fire trucks and was ready to be hosed down the sewer. It didn't help his mood that he kept catching the faint scent of her apricot shampoo and couldn't bury his face in her hair to inhale it more fully as he was tempted to do.

He took the screws she'd brought him and went back to work.

''Dad tells the story of a Christmas Eve when he had to put together a huge play kitchen for me and Karen. It had a thousand different parts and as many screws, according to Dad, and he and Mom had been at the neighbors nipping on the egg nog. Apparently it was the longest Christmas Eve on record.''

Danny grimaced, tightening down the last screw.

He could definitely sympathize with the problem and he was stone-cold sober.

Standing, he tucked the screwdriver in his hip pocket and grabbed hold of one end of the crib. "Let's see if we can get this thing upright. Don't hurt yourself," he warned when Stephanie lifted the other end.

"It's not that heavy."

They righted the bed, then made quick work of putting in the mattress, covering it with the new sheet and adding the bumper pad. Stephanie clipped the teddy bear mobile to the side rail and Danny placed the big teddy bear at the foot of the bed, the price tag still attached to its pink ribbon.

She wound the base of the mobile and they watched the miniature bears circle above the crib as the music box played a tinkling rendition of "Rock-a-bye Baby."

Instinctively he slid his arm around Stephanie's waist and pulled her close. She dipped her head to his shoulder.

"Pretty neat, huh?" Danny said, skimming his cheek across the top of her head. Her hair was silky smooth and fragrant with her shampoo.

"It's beautiful. Just perfect. She'll love it."

"Have you thought of a name yet?"

"I was thinking about naming her after my mother—Victoria—but I worry that would be too hard on Dad."

"*Victoria.*" He smiled. Instinctively he'd come close to saying *Vickie Sullivan* but stopped himself just in time. The baby would be Vickie *Gray*. No relation to him except maybe an honorary niece, which didn't sound quite right since he was going to help deliver her. "Your mom was a terrific lady. You should ask your dad what he thinks."

"Maybe I will."

"How much longer till the baby's due?"

"The middle of May. Eight weeks."

Already hanging on to his self-control by a thread, Danny suspected those eight weeks would be the longest in his life.

He swallowed hard. "What do we have to shop for next?"

Chapter Ten

Stephanie knew the preschool took field trips to the fire station. The trips didn't always happen on the days when C shift was on duty, however, and she'd figured she had a two-out-of-three chance Danny wouldn't be there when the students and teachers of Storytime Preschool showed up.

Obviously this was not a day she should buy a lottery ticket.

With a sigh, she herded her eight young charges into Station 6 through the open bay doors. It wasn't that she didn't *want* to see Danny; she wanted to see him too much. The man had become an addiction that would be hard to break, and she knew the day would come all too soon when she'd have to bite the bullet. Going cold turkey would be the easiest way; she doubted there was anything resembling a nicotine patch that would make the loss bearable.

"Stay close together, children," she reminded them. "And keep holding hands with your partner."

"There's Buttons!" True to form, Tami Malone

broke ranks, dashing forward on her own and throwing herself around the dog's neck.

"Tami!" Urging the other children along, Stephanie caught up with the girl and took her gently by the arm.

Logan Strong had Buttons well under control, and the dog looked unperturbed by Tami's energetic hug. Still, it was dangerous to have children running willy-nilly around the fire station.

"Looks like we have a dog lover visiting our station house," Logan said in his usual composed way.

With an apologetic smile at Logan, Stephanie knelt in front of the child. "What did Ms. Stephanie tell you about staying in line?"

"But I missed my doggie!" the youngster complained, her hunger to hug Buttons again palpable.

"Yes, I know, and we'll all have a chance to visit with Buttons, but you have to stay with your partner until it's your turn."

The child's lower lip protruded about an inch. "Buttons missed me, too."

"I'm sure that's true—"

"Can we slide down the fire pole?" Jason Swift asked. He gazed up toward the ceiling where the pole vanished into a circular hole, a quick means of descent for firefighters when the fire tone sounded.

"No, honey, you're too young—"

"Can we drive the fire engine?" Bobby asked.

"I'm sure the firefighters will let you sit in—"

Before she finished her sentence, both Bobby and

Jason broke for the fire truck, followed by the rest of her gang of four-year-olds.

She glanced at Logan. "I sure hope Tami's parents get her a puppy before too long. That poor little girl is absolutely dog crazy."

"So is my daughter Maddie." His smile was that of a proud father, though Stephanie knew Maddie was his wife's child by a prior marriage, which didn't seem to matter to Logan. "When she got one of Buttons' offspring, she thought she was in seventh heaven."

"She's a lucky girl in lots of ways." Including having Logan as a devoted stepfather. "Gotta corral my kids before they get into too much mischief."

With a quick smile, she hurried to round up the children again and get them back in line. Over by the ladder truck, Alice didn't appear to be having nearly as much trouble keeping order among her students. Experience apparently counted.

Or maybe Stephanie didn't have a natural inclination to manage children, which boded rather poorly for her future as a mother.

"Can I help?"

She started at the sound of Danny's voice and turned, her heart speeding up despite her efforts to remain calm. "If Buttons has some extra leashes, that would be helpful."

He chuckled, and his warm laughter did wonderful things to her insides. She'd seen him at least briefly almost every day for the past week and every time she'd gotten a quick thrill at the first sight of him.

Today was no exception. A man in uniform did that to a woman, she supposed. But in Danny's case, he looked just as good in shorts and a T-shirt. Or in nothing at all, she recalled with a sigh.

If anything, her frustration had grown even more intense since the night they'd made love. At some level, she thought Danny was having the same problem but that might be wishful thinking on her part.

How could she tell? And what on earth should she do about it even if he were as eager as she to hop back into the sack together? Or on a couch, or whatever was handy?

All of which was driving her crazy.

"I'll check with Logan," he said, "but I don't think we've got enough leashes to go around." He eyed the youngsters with some hesitancy.

"Hey, Mr. Firemens, I remember you," Bobby said. "You saved our hamsters."

"Actually your Ms. Stephanie did most of the rescuing on that little caper."

She smiled. "You can't blame it all on me. You saved Arnold, after all."

He held up his thumb. "And still have the scar to prove it."

"Have you still gots your medal?" Tami asked.

"Uh, sure I do. It's in my locker upstairs."

With a teasing grin, she said, "I thought you were going to have it mounted and hang it over the fireplace at home."

"Haven't gotten around to it yet. Been too busy

keeping tabs on a young woman I know who needs a keeper.''

"Hah! More like you spend your time bossing her around.''

"That, too,'' he agreed, his bright blue eyes teasing her. "Not that it does much good.''

"Can we see it?'' another child asked.

He shrugged. "I guess. When you go upstairs I'll show you.''

"When we go upstairs, I'm gonna slide down the pole,'' Jason announced.

"No, you're not,'' Stephanie reminded him. "The firefighters don't allow children on the fire pole.''

Jason scowled at her defiantly. She'd have to watch the child like a hawk once they were upstairs.

"Okay, kids. Who wants to sit in my fire truck?''

"I do! I do!'' they all chorused, and within moments they had turned the truck cab into a jungle gym with sound effects included.

"You did that very well,'' Stephanie commented. "Distracting the youngsters.''

"We've got a couple of probies on shift,'' he said, talking about probationary firefighters. "They'll be delighted to polish off all the fingerprints the kids leave.''

"Yeah, I bet.'' She laughed while still keeping an eye on the children. "I talked to Kim yesterday about the advertising market in Paseo.''

"And?''

"Among other things, I discovered Janice Strong, Logan's wife, works for Kim at the station.'' It had been nice to visit with both firefighter wives, although some of their questions—those about Stephanie and Danny—had been difficult to answer. "But the main thing I learned is that there's some old duffer in town who hasn't had a new thought about advertising in the past twenty years and seems to have the market locked up. Kim thinks someone with a few original ideas and a little savvy could make a living in the business."

"So are you going to give it a shot?"

She saw the challenge in his eyes and felt her own excitement. She might have left Paseo in search of adventure but she was home now, ready to dig herself some roots in the community. If there was a decent chance to make a living here at what she loved doing, she had to try.

"Absolutely," she said.

He leaned forward, his hand braced on the fire truck beside her head, his face close to hers. "Did you ever see that movie, *Backdraft?*"

She swallowed hard. At the moment her memory— or lack thereof—was the least of her troubles. The pounding of her heart appeared far more critical. "Something about firefighters?"

"Right. In it one of the firefighters got this gal up on top of the fire truck and made love to her."

"Really?" Now she remembered, all to clearly.

"How would you like to climb up there with me, Twigs?"

"I never thought those accordion-folded hose lines would be all that comfortable."

He grinned and waggled his dark brows salaciously. "I promise, you wouldn't even notice."

He was kidding. She knew he was. There were twenty preschoolers milling around the fire engines, not to mention a dozen firefighters and her own boss. He couldn't possibly want to—

"Hey!" someone shouted. "Who's that kid up in the fire tower?"

She and Danny separated, goosed by a serious case of the guilts.

Looking outside, she spotted Jason's small face peering through the second-floor window of the training tower at the back of the station, and he was waving to the onlookers below.

She groaned. "I don't know how that kid is going to make it to kindergarten, much less to adulthood."

"I'll get him," Danny said, and he trotted off toward the tower and the cluster of firefighters who had gathered beneath it.

EVERY CHILD HAD A CHANCE to try on a fire helmet and discover how heavy a firefighter's turnout coat was. When they stepped into a pair of boots, they nearly vanished out of sight. One of the volunteer mothers, who had come along on the field trip, snapped dozens of pictures to be shared in gift albums for the parents at the end of the school year.

Then they rounded up the kids and seated them at a picnic table at the back of the fire station to have their morning snacks—crackers and peanut butter Stephanie had fixed at the school earlier. Alice poured cups of juice from a thermos and Stephanie passed them out.

While Logan talked to them about having an escape route in their homes and what to do if their clothes caught on fire, the preschoolers ate their snacks.

Stephanie watched the proceedings, acutely aware of Danny, in turn, watching her. He did have the most intense way of focusing on her, as though she were the only person in the entire fire station.

Or maybe she was kidding herself and he was only trying to translate the writing on her colorful maternity blouse that read I'm Pregnant in a half-dozen different languages.

He eased up next to her. "So what's the next step in getting your business up and running?"

"Buying a computer and a color printer and designing my letterhead. I'll put together a portfolio of some of the projects I worked on in San Francisco, then I'll have to hit the pavement looking for clients."

"I don't know much about computers but I know a couple of guys who are in business for themselves. You know, old high school buddies. I could give them a call."

"Really? That would be very nice of you."

"All part of my exasperating-neighbor duties."

She laughed. "I hate to admit it, but you're not nearly as exasperating as you used to be." But definitely more sexy, as if that were possible. And more frustrating since he hadn't made love to her again and she was overcome by a raging case of shyness, reluctant to jump his bones without asking for permission.

"Be careful. I may revert to form any minute."

"I have no doubt you will." As soon as his coaching duties were over, he'd no doubt vanish from her life—except for an occasional glimpse of him through the kitchen window.

She glanced toward the children and noticed Tami had managed to latch on to Buttons. The child was petting the dog and feeding him her snack.

Stephanie stifled a groan. The poor Dalmatian was licking his chops and having little luck swallowing the sticky substance Tami had given him.

"What do you suppose peanut butter does for a dog's diet?" she asked Danny.

He followed her gaze and laughed. "He'll probably survive."

Stephanie certainly hoped so. The Dalmatian was a favorite with the children and with her.

When Logan finished his lecture about fire safety and the kids finished their snacks, Danny escorted the youngsters upstairs to the living quarters.

"Wow! That's a big TV," one of the boys said as they walked through the rec room, which was filled with a dozen recliners all facing the television.

"Well, there are a lot of us to watch it," Danny answered.

"The hard part is that there is only one remote for all those men," Stephanie chimed in.

He snapped his head around and gave her a mock glare. "Seniority rules at a fire station."

A smug grin crinkled the corners of her eyes and made him want to laugh—or kiss her senseless. Probably not a good idea here at the fire station or in front of a bunch of four-year-olds.

The little blonde Danny remembered from his visit to the school piped up. "My mommy hides the remote from my daddy if he doesn't do his chores."

"Yeah, well, we don't have that problem here. We all do our chores when we're supposed to."

"Do you take out the garbage?" blondie asked.

"Sure. Sometimes."

"And wash the dishes?"

"When it's my turn, sure." It wasn't at all clear where this conversation was heading. "We take turns cooking and cleaning, too. That's part of being a firefighter."

"Could you come teached my daddy so he doesn't get into trouble with my mommy anymore?"

He glanced at Stephanie for guidance but all he got was a helpless lift of her shoulders. "Uh, I'm sure your mom and dad will work things out."

"Why don't we let Firefighter Sullivan show us the rest of his quarters?" Stephanie suggested, finally coming to his rescue.

The tour of the kitchen didn't take long. Then they headed down the hallway past the door Greg was guarding so none of the kids inadvertently fell down the hole where the fire pole was.

"You're doing great, hotshot," Greg commented.

Standing at ease with his hands linked behind his back, he looked amused by Danny's discomfort with the kids' questions. "A regular Pied Piper."

"Next tour you get to play the heroic firefighter." It wasn't that Danny was all that uncomfortable with the kids. It's just that they were all so short. And there were so many of them. And how the hell could anybody answer their questions? What did he know about moms and dads and how they worked out their problems? His folks hadn't made the grade.

He ushered the boisterous preschoolers into his sleeping quarters, which contained a twin bed, a desk and floor-to-ceiling lockers. "Three of us use this room and we all have our own locker for our gear." He opened his to show the kids.

"You all sleep in the same bed?" a little voice asked, he wasn't sure which one.

"It's like a sleepover, dummy," another responded.

"Jason, no name calling," Stephanie reminded the child who had already lost points by climbing the training tower.

"We take turns," Danny assured them, beginning to sweat now. He could easily lose control of the situation with these short people. "There's a guy from each shift who is assigned to—"

"Ms. Stephanie, I gotta go pee," blondie announced.

Smoothly, Stephanie took the little girl's hand. "I'll take the girls and you keep track of the boys?"

"Fine." He was sure she'd been at the station often

enough to know the rest room was right down the hall from his quarters. "Don't forget to flip the sign on the door from Men to Women or you're likely to get some surprised male visitors."

"Right."

The number of kids in his room was cut in half, and a couple of the boys wanted to test out his bed. Danny figured that would be okay. It wasn't like he'd have to stand inspection anytime soon so if they messed up the covers it was no big deal. He'd just keep an eye on them to see that they didn't break their necks.

Stephanie came back with the girls and did a quick head count.

"Danny, where's Jason?"

"Who?"

"Oh, my God!" She took off running toward the rec room. "Jason! Don't you dare—"

Danny followed her. He didn't know what was up but suspected whatever was going on wasn't good. He rounded the corner in time to catch a glimpse of a small child sliding down the fire pole. An instant later, Stephanie threw herself down the same hole.

"Stephanie—no! Greg!" he bellowed, diving down the pole after her. My God, she was seven months pregnant. Why the hell hadn't Greg stopped the kid—and Stephanie. The chief would have them all up before the disciplinary board if anything happened—

His heart was in his throat by the time he landed on the ground and found Stephanie hugging the little monster who had started all this. Without thinking, he grabbed them both into the circle of his arms and held on tight, hoping his heart wouldn't fly right out of his chest, it was beating so fast and furiously.

"Don't ever do that again," he admonished them both and thanking his lucky stars someone upstairs had put a halt to the kids sliding down the pole. "You scared me to death."

"It was fun," the boy insisted, an unrepentant grin on his face.

"Are you all right?" he asked Stephanie.

"Except that you're squeezing the life out of me, of course I'm all right."

Relief mixed with the adrenaline still pumping through his veins. "What kind of an idiot stunt were you trying to pull? You could have hurt yourself badly. And the baby, too."

She looked startled that he was so upset and no less repentant than the boy. "Don't be silly, Danny. My father's a fireman. That wasn't exactly my first slide down a fire pole."

Feeling foolish, he sat back on his haunches and tried a little deep breathing to calm down. Maybe he had overreacted but it wasn't easy to convince his racing heart that there had been no danger. The image he'd had of Stephanie, broken and crumpled at the base of the pole had been too vivid for him to ignore.

She palmed his face, her hand warm and soft on his cheek. "Don't look so worried. I'm fine. Really."

"In that case—" he came to his feet, helping her up, too "—it's this young man who I have a beef with. You have any idea how upset your folks would be if you'd hurt yourself doing something stupid?''

The kid hung his head and shrugged. ''They wouldn't care.''

Stephanie cupped the back of the boy's head. ''I would, Jason. A whole lot. And so would Ms. Alice. What you did was very dangerous.''

Right on cue, Alice and the rest of the students showed up. The head teacher took over, informing Jason in no uncertain terms that he'd have a time out as soon as they got back to school. Field trip over, she hustled the youngsters to the vans.

Stephanie lingered a moment. ''That was quite an experience, wasn't it?''

''I don't think I'm cut out to be a preschool teacher,'' Danny admitted. Unable to help himself, he took her hand and threaded his fingers through hers. It felt good to hold her, even a little. She didn't object.

''Somedays I don't think I am, either.'' Walking together, they headed toward the vehicle she had arrived in. ''I guess, since you're on duty, you'll miss the childbirth class tonight.''

''No, I've got it covered. I'm taking a pager with me and if there's a problem, dispatch will give me a shout. I'll meet the crew at the scene.''

''You sure?''

''That's how all the guys handle it when their wives are pregnant.'' He realized what he'd said the moment the words were out of his mouth. Stephanie wasn't his wife. He was only her coach.

And like seeing her slide down the pole, that slip of the tongue scared him more than he cared to admit.

"DINNER IN TWO MINUTES," Logan announced from the kitchen as he set two huge pots on the counter.

Danny didn't need a second invitation to get a plate full of clam linguini, Logan's specialty. He was first in line right ahead of Jay when the phone rang in the adjacent rec room. A minute later Diaz shouted, "Sullivan! It's for you."

He cursed the caller's bad timing, and then had a panicky thought it might be Stephanie with a problem.

"Save my place, okay?" he asked Jay.

"Not a chance. If your girlfriends don't know when it's mealtime around here, it's your tough luck."

"Thanks, buddy. Remind me not to do you any favors either," he grumbled, though not with any malice. There'd be plenty of linguini to go around, although they sometimes came up short on second helpings. Whoever was calling, he wouldn't talk long.

He picked up the wall phone. "Sullivan."

"Yo, buddy. Did I interrupt your dinner?" Moose Durban laughed, knowing darn well that's exactly what he'd tried to do.

"Naw. Already ate," Danny lied. "What's up?"

"Thought we'd compare our times, see how we're doing for the triathlon."

"You mean you called me up so you can brag?" Which was exactly what Moose loved to do, part of his effort to psych his opponent out before a football game or a track meet. It wasn't going to work this time, Danny vowed.

"Not me. I just thought you'd be happy that I did my personal best in the two-mile swim at training today." Moose gave him a number that was thirty seconds faster than Danny's best time.

"You're carrying so much blubber around, you float on top of the damn ocean," he countered. Moose might be a longtime friend, but the triathlon was a blood rivalry as well as a personal salute to the buddies Danny had lost in Idaho. "I figure I'll sail right by you on my bike after you've blown a tire with all that extra load."

Moose laughed. "Hey, when are we going to get together? I dropped by the Smoke Eaters the other night and nobody had seen you in ages."

The Smoke Eaters Bar and Grill, which was around the corner from Station 6, was a hangout for firefighters from all the surrounding towns. Danny hadn't been there since Stephanie had gotten back to town.

"Yeah, well, I've been busy," he said.

"I hear you, man. It must be a girl."

It was—two of them, one inside the rounded belly of the other.

He checked his watch. He had just enough time to eat something before he left for the childbirth class. "Gotta go, Moose."

"Right, chump. Enjoy your dinner. I'll put some swim wings in the mail to you so you won't drown in my wake." His cackling laughter ended with the click of the phone as he hung up.

Danny grimaced. Forget the honor of the Paseo fire department and even the buddies he'd lost. He *really* wanted to beat the socks off Moose Durban and have the last laugh.

ONE COUPLE WAS MISSING from the class that night. The woman had gone into labor a month early and had delivered a baby boy that very morning. Although the baby was in the Intermediate Neonatal Unit, he seemed to be doing fine and would be able to go home soon.

Stephanie shuddered at the possibility of anything going wrong with her delivery or the baby. The prospect was simply too scary.

Sitting next to her at the conference table in the classroom, Danny said, "I sure hope you don't have the baby early."

"Me, too," she agreed. "Premature birth is—"

"Well, not just because it would be hazardous to her," he said, glancing at Stephanie's midsection.

"There's another reason?" That seemed the most important one to Stephanie.

"Yeah, the triathlon. You're due in what, seven weeks? The triathlon is in six weeks. I really don't want to miss that puppy."

Stephanie thought she understood. Sympathetically she said, "Because of the friends you lost?"

"That, too." He grinned. "But the truth is, my nemesis from high school days is in this race, too, and he's an overconfident jerk. I want to clean his clock."

Laughing, she said, "I'll do everything in my power not to interfere with your race. I promise." In fact, she'd probably put off delivery—and labor—as long as humanly possible.

"Thanks, Twigs. I knew you'd understand."

Maureen interrupted their conversation with a lecture on the various stages of labor, none of which sounded like fun to Danny. Then she had them move to the pillows on the floor in the middle of the room to practice relaxation exercises.

He checked the pager hooked to his belt. For the first time in his life, he wished for a huge fire to break out. Five alarms would just about do it.

No such luck, he thought as Stephanie knelt on all fours and he began to rub her back. Damn, it was going to be a long night. Thank God he had to return to the station after this instead of taking Stephanie home. The memory of what had happened after their last class created an all too familiar image in his mind.

Chapter Eleven

Stephanie handed Danny her magenta-and-goldenrod-swirled portfolio but it slipped from her fingers before he could take it. She'd spied him cooling off after one of his runs and had enticed him into the house to see the home office she'd spent the past two weeks setting up in the corner of her bedroom.

"I swear I've dropped more stuff in the past eight months than I have in my entire life," she complained as he knelt to pick up the binder. Sweat dampened his hair to a dark brown and veed down his T-shirt both front and back, creating a macho image. Sexy, too. Intriguingly so, given her high hormonal state.

"Didn't I see something about clumsiness in the pregnancy book?"

"The fact that being all thumbs is a symptom of pregnancy didn't help my mother's favorite crystal vase the other day when I dropped it."

"That's too bad." He flipped through the portfolio and smiled. "Hey, these are good."

"Of course. I'm a very talented, creative individual." Cockily she raised her chin a notch.

"And only slightly egotistical."

"Hmph. A healthy self-esteem is a necessary criteria for success in this business." She didn't take offense at his remark because she could see he was impressed with her work. *SG and Associates, Multimedia Images, Stephanie Gray, President* was a reality, including a business ID number. Now all she needed was to land a contract and produce some income to offset her substantial expenses.

"So who are these associates you're talking about?" he asked, checking out her stationery.

"The baby. I figure she and I will be spending a lot of time together in this office. I thought she deserved to be included on the letterhead." As though the baby knew she was being talked about, she stretched and shoved against Stephanie's rib cage. Stephanie winced, rubbing her hand where she felt the pressure. "Besides, it makes me seem like a big agency instead of just me and a computer mouse in my pocket."

"You okay?" Concern furrowed his brow.

"Lately the baby has been trying to work her way outside my belly by shoving my ribs apart and exiting that direction. She hasn't quite figured out she's supposed to aim south, not west."

He laughed. "She'll get the idea. It won't be long now."

"In some ways, it can't be soon enough to suit me. I'm tired of looking like a giant balloon in the Thanksgiving Day parade."

Unexpectedly he laid his hand on her stomach, the

heat of his palm instantly penetrating through her blouse. She met his gaze and felt a warmth there, too.

"You look beautiful just the way you are, Stephanie. Like a Madonna in waiting."

A flush of pleasure surged through her as he held her gaze, his eyes darkening to navy. Except for the hum of her computer, the room grew silent, the air heavy with the press of anticipation. Breath lodged in her lungs, carrying with it his subtly masculine scent, both rich and primal. At her core, she reacted in an elemental way.

She wanted him to make love to her again.

As awkward as her body felt, she'd never been more aware of every inch of her skin, never more sensitive to the lightest movement of air over her flesh. It was as though her nerve endings were closer than ever to the surface, and they ached for his touch. His caress.

The temptation to lean forward, to let their bodies collide in a sensual encounter of swollen breasts and stretched belly against the hard expanse of his chest and ribbed abdomen was nearly irresistible. The urge to feel his arms surround her converged with her need for his mouth to cover hers. To taste his flavor again.

Behind her, the bed where she'd dreamed of him all through her adolescent years mocked her. It was there that he'd made love to her a thousand times in her imagination and each time she had wanted more. Had wanted the steel-velvet length of him to fill her as no other man could.

A low moan escaped her throat.

His hand slid up her rib cage, his thumb a breath away from the swell of her breast. "Still friends, right?"

A trembling started deep inside and her gaze drifted to his lips. "Buddies. Right."

"I suppose friends—if they were real close friends—might kiss once in a while."

"Guy and girl friends."

"That's pretty much what I meant." He dipped his head toward hers, and the sweetness of his breath washed over her heated cheeks.

She reached up toward him. "I was kind of hoping that's what you had in mind."

His taste was the vibrant red and orange of every sunset she remembered, his flavor as sharp and clear as a spring morning. As his tongue stroked against hers, she rediscovered his artistry, his skill at drawing from a woman the depth of her need. She surrendered to his mastery.

Curling her fingers around the back of his neck, she drew herself closer, combing through the hair at his nape, etching the healing scar at the curve of his T-shirt and relishing the way he sculpted himself to accommodate her shape. Their concentric curves echoed each other, harmonizing like parentheses tucked one against the other.

"Stephanie?" Breathing hard, he broke the kiss and leaned his forehead against hers. "I'm all sweaty."

"I know." Her breathing was as uneven as his.

"I probably smell."

"I like how you smell. That's probably 'cause you're the guy and I'm the girl."

"You're eight months pregnant."

"I'm aware of that."

"We can't—"

"The book says we can, if we want to."

"I'd be afraid—"

"I asked my doctor. She said it's okay but she also suggested other ways—"

Uttering an oath that was both sweet and intense, he claimed her mouth again. She cherished the moment, his ardent attack on her senses. She reeled under his sensual assault, celebrating her womanhood and his potent masculinity.

He gathered the hem of her blouse upward until he found the turgid nubs of her breasts. The brush of his thumbs across the rigid tips sent a white-hot surge of desire through her, making her moan his name.

"Beautiful," he murmured before taking the nipple in his mouth.

Her adolescent fantasies paled beside the reality of Danny loving her. The bed was the same, the mattress giving beneath their combined weight as she had imagined, the sheets as cool as she remembered them.

But he was a different man. More gentle. More in control. More considerate of her needs, taking his time, making her impatient for the explosive release that she knew was only moments away.

He dragged moist kisses across her belly creating rivers of fire on her sensitive skin. Spreading her legs, he kissed the inside of her thighs, first one side and then the other.

On a cry, she arched up to him. "Danny, please—"

"Easy, Twigs. I don't want to hurt you."

The heat spiraled to the apex of her thighs. She buried her fingers in his hair and called his name again.

A rough sound came from deep in Danny's throat and he exerted all of his willpower not to take Stephanie right then. He dared not sheath himself in her welcoming flesh. She could say it was safe but he'd never forgive himself if he hurt her in any way. Or the baby.

But he could pleasure her and that would satisfy him beyond all measure.

He tasted her, and her soft cries grew more urgent. She was like silk, all hot and damp to his touch. She writhed back and forth, but he held her tight while he pleasured her more. She grabbed the sheets, fisting them in her hands as she lifted her hips to him again.

"Danny!" Her explosive release shook her body and the aftereffects rippled through him.

Catching his breath, trying to slow his wildly beating heart, he rested his head on her belly. Gently he stroked the satin curve of her stomach and down her thigh.

"You're not going to stop now, are you?" she asked.

A shuddering sigh racked his body. "Yep. I don't care what that book says or your doctor, you're too far along—"

"Daniel Sullivan, I know darn well you'll never let me live it down if you satisfied me and I didn't do the same for you."

He lifted his head. "I'm okay with it. Really."

"Oh, no, you don't, buster." She shoved him onto his back. Her eyes glittered with mirth and determination. "I'm going to have my way with you one way or the other, and you're going to enjoy every darn minute of it."

"Stephanie, you don't have to—"

Too late. She was already kissing him in the most intimate way possible. No amount of willpower would have been strong enough to make him shove her away. How could he have not known years ago what a sensual woman Stephanie was? Or maybe he'd sensed it and that was the reason he'd kept his distance. He didn't know the answer. For the moment, the sweet friction of her lips and tongue was all he could think about.

Then her hand replaced her mouth, the friction just as sweet and smooth, and he couldn't think at all as his breathing grew harsher. The pulsing started deep inside and erupted like a banked fire sped out of control when oxygen fed the flames.

Numb and sated, he lay there for a long time, Stephanie's head resting on his chest. *Friends.* More than that, he realized, but he still wasn't sure how to define their relationship.

Nor did he know what he could offer to Stephanie without the risk of hurting her as badly as his mother had suffered by his father's desertion.

More than once Danny's mother had said he looked much like his father. He'd always feared he was like the man in other ways, too—unable to commit to a woman he loved. Twice in his life he'd thought he was in love—once in high school and once in Idaho. In each case he'd awakened one morning in a panic, claustrophobic at the idea of spending the rest of his life tied to the same woman.

Like his father had echoed in his head.

God, he couldn't do that to her.

Already betrayed once by a man, Stephanie deserved better than that.

Vaguely he became aware of a car arriving at the house followed by footsteps on the driveway and then the back door opening.

"Stephanie, honey! I'm home."

At the sound of her father's voice, she shot off the bed. So did Danny. Frantically he scooped up his running shorts, tugged them on, and grabbed for his T-shirt. The still-sweaty shirt stuck to his skin as he tried to pull it on over his head with one hand while at the same time he stuck his feet into his cross-training shoes. He'd just righted himself when Harlan Gray appeared in the doorway.

"Oh, hi, Danny. I didn't know you were here."

Beaded sweat formed on Danny's forehead. In about two seconds he'd be the target of a firing squad—or a shotgun. "Yes, sir. Stephanie was showing me her new office."

"Nice setup she's got, isn't it?"

In a jerky movement, Stephanie finger combed her

short hair and smoothed down her blouse. "You're home early." Her smile was a little too bright, her voice too high pitched. Her cheeks flamed with color, matching her vibrant red-and-yellow blouse.

The chief's gaze touched on his daughter and her disheveled appearance, then slid to the mussed bed-clothes and rumpled sheets.

"Yes, well, I had a meeting in the north end of town and thought I'd drop by to have lunch with you."

Danny cleared his throat. "Well, I'll be on my way—"

"Don't leave on my account, son. I'll, uh, just fix myself a cup of coffee and a sandwich."

"I'll be right with you, Dad."

"No need. You carry on with whatever—" He made a vague gesture with his hand. "I'll be in the kitchen if you need me."

As soon as Harlan left the room, Stephanie sat down heavily on the end of the bed. In a hoarse whisper, she said, "I can't believe my father practically caught us in the act."

"I'm sorry, Stephanie. God, I'm really sorry." He speared the fingers of both hands through his hair. "I'll tell your dad it was all my fault. I took advantage of you."

Her head snapped up. Her lips were swollen from his kisses, her cheeks still red from both embarrassment and the brush of his whiskers. "You'll do no such thing. What we did was consensual on all counts—unless I was the one taking advantage of you.''

His lips quirked into a smile. ''Face it, I'm a weak guy.''

Taking his hand, she ran his knuckles along her cheek. ''You'd better go now, hotshot, before I take advantage of you again with my dad right outside the door.''

''Probably wouldn't be a good career advancement move on my part.'' Bending over, he kissed her lightly on the lips. He *was* weak when it came to Stephanie. He wasn't sure how that had happened or when. She used to be such a pesky kid, always under foot. Now he simply knew, eight months pregnant or not, he couldn't resist her. ''See you tomorrow morning for our walk?''

She nodded and patted her tummy. ''We'll be ready.''

A WEEK LATER, Danny and Jay Tolliver were using push brooms to sweep up the debris they'd brought down while breaking through a ceiling to suppress an attic fire started by frayed electrical wiring. Soggy plaster covered the floor in the damaged kitchen. If the crew hadn't protected the furniture with a salvage cover, the damage would have been worse.

''So how's your wife's pregnancy coming along?'' Danny asked idly, although his question wasn't at all casual. He kept wondering if his sexual attraction to Stephanie was abnormal, her being so far along in her pregnancy. But that wasn't something you could outright ask, not even in the childbirthing class. Nor could he bring himself to discuss other troubling thoughts he'd been having in a public arena.

"She's good. She complains she's getting as big as a house, of course, but she's healthy and that's all that counts."

"Guess being, uh, large like that can turn a guy off, huh?"

"Are you kidding? Kim's never been more sexy. It's like we're on our honeymoon again, except she's still working nights at the radio station." Jay shot him a grin that had once made him a big money winner at the annual hospital bachelor auction supporting the burn unit.

Leaning on his broom, Danny watched Jay work for a minute. "Are you scared?"

"Scared? Of what?"

"Of something going wrong with the delivery, something bad happening to Kim."

"Oh, that. I'm not just scared, Sullivan. I'm terrified." He stopped sweeping, too, and assumed the same lazy pose of leaning on his broom that Danny had chosen. "But you know what's really got me waking up in the middle of the night?"

Danny shook his head. It couldn't be much worse than his own worries over Stephanie, and the two of them weren't even married.

"That I won't be a good enough father. That I'll blow it like my old man did. That's what gives me nightmares."

"So how do you know you will be okay?"

"I guess you have to decide to give it your best shot and let the cards fall where they will. Kim keeps telling me there's never been a perfect parent in the whole history of mankind so we shouldn't beat ourselves up over it. We'll make mistakes but as long as the little guy knows we love him, everything will come out okay."

"You're having a boy, huh?"

"Yeah. Kim wants him to look just like me."

"With your ugly puss? You're telling me she'd wish that on some poor little kid?"

"Hey, what can I say? She loves me." With a satisfied grin, he went back to pushing his broom.

Danny envied Jay his confidence. He made having a baby and parenthood sound so damn simple. And maybe it was when the couple was married and loved each other.

Grabbing a shovel, Danny scooped up some of the debris and tossed it out the back door to a collection spot. He wasn't in the same position as Jay. He and Stephanie weren't married. He wasn't even sure how he felt about her, except that he had trouble staying away from her and his dreams about her were getting downright X-rated. And he didn't have a clue how she felt about him. She wasn't repulsed but she sure hadn't dropped any hints about marriage. At least none that he had heard.

Meanwhile, he'd been mentally toying with the notion that under different circumstances, if the timing had been different, the baby Stephanie was carrying could have been his.

That's where things got a little tricky. Because lately he'd been thinking that would be a damn good idea.

TWO WEEKS OF PHONE CALLS, pounding the pavement and making presentations, and she'd finally done it. She had her first advertising contract. She'd talked Boutique Bagels into a summer-sandwich-special to boost their lunchtime volume. There would be print ads and local radio spots to promote the featured items. In contrast to the media packages she'd set in motion at Edgar's firm, this contract was small potatoes.

But it was a beginning.

Stephanie whipped her Honda into the employee parking lot behind Station 6 and squeezed herself out from behind the wheel. Another few days and she wouldn't be able to fit in her car at all.

But for now, she wanted to share her good news with Danny, and she didn't want to wait for tomorrow when he'd have his day off.

The late-afternoon sun slanted through the open bay doors, catching Engine 62 in a column of light as it backed into its assigned position following a run and came to a stop.

Stephanie's heart seized as she realized during all of her excitement, Danny had been putting his life on the line fighting a fire somewhere in Paseo. She hadn't given him or the danger he faced daily a thought. Selfishly, she'd only been thinking about herself.

She met him when he stepped down from the truck and reached up on tiptoe, kissing him lightly. "Welcome home."

Color bloomed in his cheeks beneath a smudge of soot. "Hey, I don't get welcomed home like that often."

"The department probably needs to hire cheerleaders so you fellows won't feel neglected."

"I'll put the idea in the suggestion box. The chief will love it. He'll probably insist they wear those revealing short skirts." He grinned at her mischievously, and she knew it hadn't been a bad fire. No one had been injured.

Her sense of relief almost made her forget why she'd dropped by the station. "I got my first contract."

Taking off his helmet, he tossed it back into the cab of the truck. "For an advertising job?"

"You bet. Boutique Bagels down on Broadway."

"Way to go, Twigs!" He picked her up under her arms and twirled her around.

She gasped with both delight and surprise. "Put me down! You're going to drop me."

"No way, sweetheart. What we've gotta do is celebrate your sale. Up on top of the truck—" he started to boost her up to the rack of accordion folded hose at the top of the truck "—and we'll do the deed—"

"We'll do no such thing!"

Jay Tolliver sauntered over from Engine 62, his turnout coast smudged with soot, too. "*Backdraft* was a great movie, wasn't it?"

"No. It destroyed the firefighters' honorable image," she complained.

Danny ignored the exchange between Stephanie and Jay and looked up at the coiled hoses, assessing the situation. "I suppose if you fell off the truck, it'd be like Humpty Dumpty and I'd never get you put back together again."

Unable to help herself, she laughed. "I'd rather not test out just how fragile I am."

"Understandable." His hands closed gently around her shoulders and he drew her closer. "How 'bout we celebrate with a kiss right here."

She wanted to object. She really meant to. But before she knew what was happening, his mouth covered hers and she forgot all about the firefighters drifting around the bay area, checking their gear, getting ready for the next fire they'd have to fight.

She drew a shaky breath when he finally released her. Low and raspy as though he'd inhaled more smoky air than was good for him, he said, "I'm proud of you, Twigs. I knew you could make a success of your business."

She basked in the glow of his praise for the few seconds before his cohorts began to razz him for fraternizing with the chief's daughter.

Knowing the crews had work to do, and embarrassed by their very public kiss, Stephanie ducked out of the station. Danny would come by in the morning for their walk—not that she could go far these days with her protruding tummy arriving at any new destination well ahead of the rest of her.

She drove home and turned into her driveway, noting there was a new Jaguar parked at the curb. She frowned as she got out of her Honda. It was the middle of the afternoon. Her father wasn't home yet.

A troubling unease crept down her spine.

Without looking in the direction of the unfamiliar car, she headed for the back door.

She heard or sensed him behind her and picked up her pace.

"Stephanie, wait."

Her heart thudded against her ribs and she came to a halt, then turned to greet the father of her child, Edgar Bresse the Third.

Chapter Twelve

"What on earth are you doing here?" she asked.

"I've missed you, Stephanie." Impeccably dressed, as always, his blond hair perfectly styled, he shoved his hands into the pockets of his hand-tailored slacks. "Isn't that a good enough reason for me to drop by to see you?"

Almost three months without a word and now he shows up out of the blue, driving three hours down Highway 101 from San Francisco?

Stephanie had the desperate feeling Edgar's visit wasn't as benign as he let on. "You came a long way for a social visit without calling first."

"I was afraid you'd tell me not to come."

"You're right. I would have."

"Come on, Stephanie. We had a lot going for us. You can't simply toss that aside—"

"Me?" Her voice rose in surprise. "You're the one who did the tossing. After I told you I was pregnant, you didn't want to have anything more to do with me." *Or my baby.*

"I owe you an apology for my behavior. I got a

little panicky, you know? Like I wasn't exactly ready to settle down yet.''

She eyed him skeptically. ''Are you saying you're ready now?''

Instead of answering, he strolled back to the front porch. In the slanting rays of the late-afternoon sun, he looked like a blond Adonis, an image that no longer held any appeal for her. Why, she wondered, had she ever thought she loved this man?

He picked up a long, white florist box. ''Maybe this will help make up for what I did to you.''

Against her better judgment, she accepted the box. ''Flowers aren't going to cut it, Edgar.'' Among other things, she'd fallen hard for someone else and had come to realize Edgar wasn't worth a single one of the tears she'd shed over him.

''Just take a look, okay?'' He eased the lid off the box. ''I remembered how much you loved roses. Think of these as the first installment of my apology.''

It was all she could do not to gasp at the mass of three dozen long-stem red roses. The extravagant scent filled the air making it almost too rich to breathe. ''I don't want your flowers or anything else from you, Edgar. Whatever you're after, it's too late now.''

His cheeks flushed a bright red and, in an uncharacteristically evasive mannerism, his gaze shot away from hers to the climbing roses growing up a trellis beside the front porch. ''I think it's worth discussing, don't you?''

Something wasn't adding up. He'd made it abundantly clear before she left San Francisco that he had no further interest in her and even less interest in their baby.

"To what do we owe your sudden change of heart?"

He glanced around the yard and toward the neighbors' houses where not a soul was in sight, not even the flick of a curtain to suggest someone was watching them.

"Could we take this conversation inside? A little privacy would be nice."

Stephanie was torn. On the one hand, he'd rejected her when she'd been vulnerable and that had hurt. Deeply. For that reason alone, she had no further desire to see him. Danny's arrival in her life was an added bonus, however temporary that might be. It had made her see Edgar as a shallow, cardboard cutout of a man compared to Danny.

Still, Edgar was her baby's father. She didn't have the right to keep him away from his little girl.

Though, for the life of her, she couldn't fathom why—after his adamant rejection of the baby—he'd want to be involved with the child at all. Or why he'd bring her flowers.

With a taut gesture, she invited him to follow her inside through the back door.

She hadn't put the breakfast dishes away that morning and they cluttered the sink. An empty orange juice carton still sat on the table. She felt like scurrying around to tidy things up. Edgar was a neat freak, making her feel guilty if she didn't clean up a mess the moment it happened.

In contrast, Danny had never once criticized her housekeeping skills or her lack of interest in the pursuit of improving those talents.

Dropping the florist box on the kitchen table, she kept on walking into the living room where dust covered the furniture to a depth of two inches, or so it seemed to her as she looked around through Edgar's eyes. Starting a business was a full-time job, she reminded herself, and she'd had little energy left over for domestic activity. If he'd wanted neat and tidy along with a red carpet rolled out, he'd come to the wrong place.

Scooping up a day-old newspaper from the couch, she refolded it and set it on the table on top of a disorderly stack of her father's firefighter magazines.

"My parents send their regards."

She doubted his parents had given her a single thought in the past few months. "Tell them hello for me, too."

"You're looking well, Stephanie."

Instinctively she linked her hands across her distended belly, and his gaze followed her gesture. "Thank you. You're looking debonair, as always."

A faint smile lifted his narrow lips. "The baby? Everything is going along as expected? All healthy and normal?"

"So far, so good." Neither of them had taken a seat and they stood on opposite ends of the coffee table but the gulf between them after all these months was far wider than a mere few feet. "You didn't come here to indulge in idle chitchat, Edgar, and I sincerely doubt your change of heart includes a proposal."

Rather than sitting down, which would leave her in the power position of height, he paced across the room to the fireplace and took a lord-of-the-manor pose with his legs wide apart, his hands clasped behind his back.

"I believe—for the sake of the baby—we ought to put aside our differences. I *am* prepared to marry you."

Her jaw went slack. Months ago when she announced her pregnancy she'd hoped Edgar would propose. But not now. She no longer wanted to marry him and wouldn't have him if he came gift-wrapped with a bow around his neck.

"You're *prepared?*" She had to laugh, albeit with a certain amount of bitterness. "That's probably the least romantic proposal I've ever heard of and the answer is an unequivocal thanks but no thanks."

"Stephanie…" He brushed at an imaginary piece of dirt on the sleeve of his shirt. "Look, I had intended to take you out to a nice dinner, reestablish our relationship and then propose, hopefully amid music and candlelight. But the reception you've given me hasn't exactly been warm."

"Hah! You're damn lucky I didn't bar the doors and toss boiling oil on you out the window." His nervous mannerisms, the way he couldn't quite meet her gaze, suggested he hadn't had a change of heart at all. Only his agenda had changed but she didn't know why.

The fact that he'd show up after all these months and then *lie* to her sent a familiar dart of betrayal through her. Whatever his words, at his core Edgar was still rejecting her…and her baby.

Thank goodness she'd already decided to move on with her life without him.

When she gave no indication of relenting, he drew himself up to precise military-school attention and squared his shoulders. "Really, Stephanie, dear, you didn't used to be so peevish."

"Blame it on the pregnancy, if you like, but the answer is still no. I have no interest in marrying you or anyone else anytime soon." Particularly since the man she'd fallen in love with didn't reciprocate her feelings. "I'm getting along just fine as I am. And I'd like you to leave. Now."

With flawless timing, Harlan Gray chose that moment to arrive home from the office. He came in through the back door and walked into the living room.

"Stephanie, whose car is parked—" He halted abruptly, eyeing their guest with surprise and no great pleasure. The few times they'd met, Harlan had expressed little eagerness for Edgar as Stephanie's boyfriend. Her unintended pregnancy had certainly not endeared the man to her father.

"I didn't expect to see you here," Harlan said.

Striding across the room, Edgar extended his hand. "Good to see you, Mr. Gray. You're looking well."

When Harlan didn't accept his hand, Edgar let his fall to his side.

Harlan's gaze darted to Stephanie. ''Is everything all right?''

''Edgar was just leaving, Dad.''

''Actually I had hoped to take Stephanie out to dinner, sir. Renew our acquaintance. Talk over our future.''

Acquaintance? Stephanie's gaze shot to her father, and she saw a muscle flex in his jaw. Her big belly suggested her relationship with Edgar had been far more than a casual acquaintance.

''Sorry,'' she said to Edgar. ''We're having frozen macaroni for dinner tonight. I wouldn't want to miss that and there's only enough for Dad and me. Good-bye, Edgar.''

He forced a strained smile. ''Perhaps tomorrow then.''

''Can't squeeze it in. I plan to be busy cleaning toilets. You know how I love to be domestic.''

His smile turned into a scowl. Reaching into his pocket, he produced a small, blue-velvet box and placed it with a determined snap on the cluttered coffee table. ''Maybe this will change your mind, give you a glimpse of what I can offer you. I'll drop by in the morning for your answer.''

He whirled, and Harlan stepped out of his way as Edgar marched into the kitchen. The outside door slammed behind him.

Stephanie exhaled and eased the tension in her

shoulders, although she couldn't manage to slow the pulse beating in her throat.

"What was that all about?" her father asked.

"Edgar has decided we ought to get married."

Raising his eyebrows, Harlan said, "I gather you told him no."

"Emphatically."

He crossed the room and took Stephanie in his arms, hugging her. "Are you sure, sweetie? You used to think you loved him."

"I was a fool and fell in love with the glitter, Dad. There wasn't any substance." Why had it taken so long for her to realize that? Perhaps she'd needed to see the contrast between Danny's enduring nature and Edgar's fake facade before she could fully appreciate the difference.

"You're going to be fine. You'll see. I never did much like that young man."

He patted her back as she rested her head on his shoulder, and she remembered all the times her father had reassured her, promising to make everything all right again. In the long run, even after the death of her mother, his promises had come true.

"Are you going to take a look at what's in the box he left?"

"Not much point when I'm going to give it back."

Cocking his head, he eyed her skeptically. "You're not just a tiny bit curious?"

In spite of herself, she giggled. Her father knew her too well. "It's probably huge, exorbitantly expensive and wouldn't suit my taste at all."

"Good. Let's look." He reached for the ring box.

"Dad!"

"You ought to at least know what you're giving up."

Reluctance warred with curiosity. A moment passed before curiosity won, and she lifted the lid of the box.

The glittering diamond had to be a full five karats, the solitaire surrounded by a dozen smaller stones worth in combination nearly as much as the single stone.

She showed her father then snapped the box closed, not dazzled by Edgar's show of affluence in the way she once would have been. It would be no sacrifice to give him back a gaudy ring that she'd be afraid to wear in public for fear she'd be mugged.

"I'm not giving up a thing, Dad. Edgar doesn't love me, and that's all I really want from the man I marry."

She thought of Danny, and regret slid through her. He didn't love her either. But he did care, she knew that much. She also knew if he ever did fall in love, a woman's heart would be safe in his hands.

DANNY HEADED HOME AS SOON as his replacement from B shift arrived at the station to relieve him in the morning.

He changed into his running shorts at his house and trotted over to Stephanie's for their morning walk. Afterward, he'd do some wind sprints at the high school track then go for a 10K run. With only three days until the triathlon, his training had peaked. Now he only had to stay loose and not overdo.

Rapping his knuckles on Stephanie's back door, he went inside without waiting for an invitation.

His breath lodged in his lungs at the sight of her standing in the middle of the kitchen wearing a bright maternity blouse, her walking shorts and holding a huge bouquet of red roses in her arms. A sudden stab of jealously punctured the image of her waiting expressly for him.

"Where did those come from?"

She hummed an unintelligible sound. "Edgar dropped by last night."

"Edgar? What did he want?"

"He, uh, proposed."

That news slammed into Danny's gut, almost doubling him over in pain. A man who shows up with that many roses in hand is serious about getting married.

Fury replaced the pain lancing through his stomach, and he clenched his hands into fists. He wanted to find this Edgar jerk, knock him around a little, and tell him that he couldn't have Stephanie. She belonged to *him,* Danny Sullivan. The same guy who'd gone to all those childbirth classes with her. The one who had lugged the crib into the house and put it together for the baby. The one who had made love to Stephanie—twice—after Edgar had dumped her. And he wanted to do it again.

But he didn't have the right. She'd loved Edgar

first. She was carrying *his* baby, not Danny's. He'd lost them both.

He gritted his teeth. "What the hell took him so long to decide to marry you?"

She opened her mouth to respond but the front doorbell chimed, interrupting her. Nobody came to the Gray's front door except strangers. Friends and neighbors used the back.

She glanced toward the living room. "That's probably him now."

"Great," Danny muttered. "I'll just slip out the back and—"

"No. I'd like you to stay."

Something in her eyes brought him up short, a mix of anxiety and alarm. "What's wrong?"

"I told Edgar yesterday that I wasn't interested in marrying him or anyone else." The doorbell rang again. "He didn't take the news real well. Dad isn't here and I'm afraid—"

Relief propelled him past Stephanie. "I'll get the door."

"Danny, I don't want you to start anything. I can handle—"

He yanked open the door. The man standing there was everything Danny wasn't—smooth, sophisticated and, from the cut of his clothes, wealthy. *Stephanie turned him down!* Danny nearly jumped up and clicked his heels together.

"Whatever you're selling, Stephanie doesn't want any."

Edgar narrowed his baby blues at Danny. "Who are you?"

With amazing agility, given her advanced pregnancy, Stephanie wedged herself between them. "Edgar, this is my neighbor, Danny Sullivan. Edgar Bresse, my former employer."

The introduction didn't appear to please Edgar. "I'd like to speak to you alone, Stephanie."

"I think I made myself clear last night. I have no interest in marrying you. If you'll wait a moment, I'll get the ring—" She slipped back into the living room.

Grinning foolishly, Danny leaned against the doorjamb, his arms folded across his chest. *You blew it, rich boy. You could have had—*

Edgar caught him off guard and brushed past him. "I don't believe you fully understand the situation, Stephanie."

She held out a small box to him, the ring, Danny realized. He'd bet it was a doozy and still she didn't want it—or Edgar. *Good girl!*

Without taking the box, Edgar continued. "It's not going to be easy for you to raise the baby as a single mother with limited resources."

"If you've decided to provide financial support, I appreciate the offer but I don't need your help."

Danny wanted to tell him there were others around who would be happy to take care of her if that's what she needed. Which she didn't. She'd do fine on her own.

"That's not the point. As you're aware, my parents are extraordinarily proud of the Bresse name and our family's history, being a part of the gold rush, helping to turn California into a thriving state.''

"Your ancestors lined their pockets with the hard-earned gold the miners had sweated to dig out of the ground," she said mildly. "Then they cheated land owners who'd been burned out in the big fire."

His flawless forehead furrowed into a frown. "In any event, they always regretted they couldn't have more than one child. For four generations, the Bresse line has been a powerful force in California. Naturally they feel they have a vested interest in the upbringing of the fifth generation—our child."

Visibly paling, Stephanie sat down in the nearest chair.

Danny hurried to her side, resting his hand on her slender shoulder. "Are you okay?"

She nodded but didn't take her eyes off Edgar. "What are you trying to say?"

"If you're not willing to marry me, my mother suggests we'd be doing you a favor if, when the time comes, we take the baby off your hands."

"Take the baby—"

"Now wait a minute," Danny interjected. "You can't come waltzing in here—"

"Stay out of this while Stephanie hears me out. This is the most reasonable course of action for both you and our baby. Look around you." He aimed a particularly disdainful look at Danny. "The Bresse family has a hundred—no, a thousand times the financial resources you can offer the child. He'd have private schools, trips abroad, the best college—"

"It's a girl. If you're looking for another Edgar for your family tree, you won't find him here."

Edgar hesitated for a fractional beat. "All right, a girl, who would have all those same advantages. Social position. Admission to the best clubs. Welcomed in influential circles by the very best people."

"I think you'd better leave," Danny said tautly.

"You have no interest at all in my baby, do you?" Stephanie said. "You were planning all along to hand her over to your mother to raise—over my objections, if necessary."

"If you want the truth, no, I don't have any desire for a baby cluttering up my life. But I do need continued access to my trust fund, which my mother controls. The advertising business isn't lucrative enough to support my tastes."

"You're doing this for *money?*" Stephanie gasped.

He shrugged indulgently. "The baby would benefit by this arrangement, too. She'd have everything she needs. The best clothes. Dancing lessons. You name it—"

"What about love? Do you really think that cold-blooded fish of a mother of yours is *capable* of love? Look what she did to you."

Based on the red splotches on his face, Edgar's blood pressure had topped three hundred. "Be careful what you say, *Miss* Gray. The Bresse family has access to thousands of attorneys, high-priced attorneys who could prove you an unfit mother with no more than a snap of their fingers."

"You wouldn't!" she gasped.

"That's it!" Taking Edgar by the arm, Danny man-handled him toward the door. For all his fancy duds, he had as much muscle power as an empty fire hose.

"You're not being reasonable, either of you," he said over his shoulder.

Her face flushed, Stephanie awkwardly levered herself to her feet. "Don't come back, Edgar. I'll get a restraining order if I have to. The mighty Bresse name doesn't carry any clout in Paseo del Real." She tossed the ring box toward him.

He caught it in midair. "I'll leave—for now. But I have rights, too," he warned from the porch. "You can't keep me away from that baby. I'm its father."

Chapter Thirteen

"What am I going to do?" Panic and her false bravado stole the strength from Stephanie's knees. She sank back onto the chair as Edgar's parting threat pealed like the voice of doom in her head. "He's going to take my baby."

"No, he's not." Kneeling, Danny wrapped his arms around her. "There's no way I'll let him take her. I swear it."

"You don't realize how influential the Bresse family is in the Bay area. They have more money than God. I could fight them here in Paseo—people know me, my father—but up north—"

"Shh, we'll think of something."

"He'll sue for custody. He's her *father!* I won't be able to stop him. Then he'll—" She choked on the fear that threatened to strangle her. "He'll kidnap her."

"Easy, sweetheart, you're getting way ahead of yourself." Danny stroked her face, wiping away her tears then soothed his hand over her belly. "You don't want to upset little Vickie over something that might never happen, do you?''

In spite of herself, her lips quivered with a smile. ''Vickie?''

''Yeah, you said... Is the name okay with your dad?''

She nodded. ''He likes the idea.''

''There, you see?'' He patted her stomach again. ''You hear that, Vickie? Now you listen to ol' Danny here. Nobody, I mean *nobody,* is going to take you away from your mom. You got that?''

The baby shifted, pressing against Stephanie's ribs and her bladder at the same time. Not Victoria or Torrie but Vickie. Stephanie thrilled at the thought Danny had chosen her child's nickname for her.

Danny looked at her in wonder. ''I felt her move. I think she heard me.''

''I think so, too.'' Danny's was the masculine voice Vickie heard most often. His gentle baritone. His laughter. Little wonder the baby responded when he spoke to her so intimately with such love in his voice. Stephanie never failed to respond with the same depth of feeling. ''But I don't see how I can protect her.''

''We'll find a way.'' He sat back on his haunches, his hand still resting, warm and reassuring, on her belly. ''I've got a friend who's an attorney. He used to be with the department but got himself hurt on the job. He'll be able to figure out something, I'm sure of it.''

Stephanie wished she were as confident as Danny. ''There isn't much time before—''

''Hey, Vickie isn't due to make an appearance for what, another ten days? I'll go see Jackson this morning, see what he says. There'll be plenty of time to file a restraining order or do whatever it takes to keep ol' Edgar away from you—and Vickie.''

''I don't know…''

He silenced her with a kiss that took her breath away. He claimed her mouth and her soul as though with a single kiss he intended to show her that all the promises he made would come true. Her fear dissolved and love rose to replace it, filling her more completely that she had thought possible. And giving her hope.

''Trust me,'' he whispered.

''I do.'' With her heart and with her baby's future.

He gave her a cocky grin as he stood. ''I promised your dad I'd be your coach, and I'm not going to let some rich playboy run either of us off the field.''

With a quick grin, he jogged out of the house.

I promised your dad. Stephanie felt a crack form in her heart and begin to widen.

After all these weeks, Danny was still helping her out of a false sense of obligation to her father.

Stephanie wept for the loss of hope she'd so recently harbored of dreams coming true.

DANNY'S FRIEND, LeRoy Jackson, had made the situation pretty clear. There was only one possible way for Stephanie to protect the baby from Edgar's grasp if the Bresse family wanted to press the issue. Her best hope.

Standing outside Stephanie's house, Danny jammed his hands into his pockets. He'd only been gone a couple of hours but everything was about to change. Now the big question was, would Stephanie go for the idea or take her chances fighting Edgar on her own?

Hell, she deserved better than the only choice he had to offer. *Him.* She'd likely turn him down flat. For Vickie's sake, he wasn't going to let her.

The front door opened. "What are you doing out there standing on the sidewalk like you're lost?" Stephanie called to him.

Trying to build up more courage than it takes to go into a burning building when there's no water in the hose.

Slowly he walked toward the porch. Sweat edged down his spine and pooled under his arms. Man, he couldn't remember ever going into her house via the front door. Somehow, this time, it seemed appropriate.

"I talked to the attorney."

"And?" She looked hopeful.

His mouth felt dry. "He came up with a possible solution to your problem." Though Danny wasn't sure she'd be pleased with the prospect.

"Come in. Please." She opened the door wider. "Tell me what he said."

Danny had been in this house a thousand times. Maybe more. He'd always felt at home. But not now. Everything looked unfamiliar, as though his world had shifted onto a new axis. Or was about to.

"Well?" she prodded.

"Uh, paternity rights are well accepted now, so Edgar's position is pretty strong."

"I know that. So what does your friend say I have to do?"

He hesitated, swallowing hard. "He says there's a presumption in law that a baby belongs to a woman's husband unless he disputes the issue." Danny wouldn't ever dispute that. He already loved Vickie, and no matter what happened, that wouldn't change.

"Edgar's not my husband but he is—"

"You need to marry someone else before the baby is born."

She gaped at him. "I what?"

"I figured you and me—" He gestured vaguely. "We could get married."

"You're kidding!"

Damn, it hurt that she'd rejected the notion so out of hand. She could have at least given him a chance to plead his case. But he wasn't about to give up easily, not when it came to Stephanie or the baby.

"I see it this way. We can take a run down to the county courthouse this afternoon, get the license and the three-day waiting period will be over on Sunday. We can get married after the triathlon."

It looked as if she'd had a sudden onset of lockjaw, her mouth was hanging so far open. It took several full heartbeats before she got her mouth working again, every moment a painful wait for Danny.

"I don't think this is a good idea," she said.

"My friend Jackson says it's your best shot at

keeping Edgar and his old lady out of your hair. You put my name down as Vickie's father on the birth certificate and with us married, it'll be tough for him to get a judge to order any blood tests without your permission.''

Visibly stunned and looking pale, she shook her head. ''I can't tell you how fortunate I feel as a woman to have had *two* proposals in the past two days from men who have no real interest in marrying me.''

''Stephanie,'' he said quietly, feeling like a jerk and knowing he was making a mess of things. Hell, he'd never proposed to anyone before and knew darn well he was no great shakes as a husband prospect. But he'd give his right arm to make it all right for her and the baby.

''Look at it this way. You'll be keeping your options open. You have to attack a fire from all directions, you can appreciate that. We'll start with this and maybe somebody else will come up with a better idea later. We'll consult another attorney. Meanwhile, if we go ahead and get the license, you'll have me as a backup position.''

''You're only doing this because you feel obligated to my father.''

''Hey, that's not why. I mean, we're already friends, aren't we? That's more than some couples can say.''

She bristled like a cat threatening to attack. ''How thoughtful of you—another in my growing list of truly romantic reasons to get married.''

''Give me a break, huh? I'm trying to do the right

thing here.'' Danny backpedaled. He'd said some- thing that had upset her but he wasn't sure what. He knew darn well, under normal circumstances, she wouldn't be jumping up and down to marry him—a guy who couldn't promise commitment. He'd never even come close. But she didn't have to be quite so ticked off about his proposal.

Turning away, Stephanie's shoulders shook as she fought off a sob. Danny couldn't possibly know how much his words had hurt her. Marriage to him would mean the world to her but not this way. Not when he felt forced into the situation by her own stupidity of getting involved with a man like Edgar, who hadn't deserved her love.

She didn't want Danny to rescue her; she wanted him to *love* her.

Danny's arms slid around her, encompassing her baby, too, and he rested his cheek against her head. His breath blew warm and sweet against her face.

''Come on, Stephanie. Let's get the license. What can it hurt?''

What indeed, she wondered, except that she'd suf- fer a little more heartache by knowing he never in- tended for their marriage to be real.

''You can't help being bossy, can you?''

''Nope, it's part of my nature.''

In spite of everything, she smiled. That was a part of him she loved, too.

A MOCK-ADOBE BUILDING housed the county court- house. Danny parked his SUV in a parking lot shaded by jacaranda trees in full bloom, their purple flowers scattered across the hoods of nearby cars like colorful raindrops from a spring shower.

He'd taken Stephanie by the hospital first to get the results of both of their recent blood tests, hers when she had preregistered for the baby's delivery and his when he'd last donated blood, a couple of months ago.

Now came the all important visit to the license bureau. She'd been so quiet the whole time, he was afraid she would balk and refuse to go inside.

Hopping out of the truck, he rounded the back and opened her door. "Out you come." He lifted his arms to help her down.

She stared at him for the longest time, her expression unreadable. "Are you sure you want to do this?"

"Yep. I like the idea of outsmarting pretty-boy Bresse." Despite the nerves twisting through his gut, Danny strained to sound nonchalant. "Besides, I'll have plenty of time after the triathlon to get married. We can even go out to dinner."

Her eyes fluttered closed as though she were experiencing some discomfort. When she opened them again he saw a sheen of tears had dimmed the golden sparks in her hazel eyes.

"I'm sorry, Danny. For your sake, I wish there were some other choice." She laid her hands on his shoulders.

Helping her from the truck, he cursed himself for not being a better man, the *right* man for Stephanie and the baby. "Come on, Twigs, cheer up. Folks will think I'm forcing you to marry me. Getting a marriage license is supposed to be a happy occasion.''

''I'll keep that in mind.'' The absence of a real smile wasn't encouraging.

He kept his arm around her waist as they walked into the courthouse. She'd developed a cute little waddle in recent weeks, and her hip bumped up against his. The way the baby preceded her by a full stride, and how Stephanie had to arch her back to keep from toppling on her face, Danny was always afraid she would lose her balance. He sure didn't want her to fall, not in her condition. He wasn't prepared to do an emergency delivery on the steps of the courthouse no matter how many childbirth classes he'd taken.

In the license bureau, a smiling, round-faced clerk perched on a stool behind the counter merrily stamped completed forms for a lovey-dovey couple who couldn't stop kissing and giggling.

''See, that's how we're supposed to act,'' Danny whispered as he picked up forms from a holder near the door.

Stephanie rolled her eyes. ''I haven't giggled like that since I was fourteen.''

''We could do the kissing part.'' He leaned over and gave her the long, hungry kiss he'd been aching for since he'd proposed—and she'd accepted, however reluctantly. A man needed to seal an agreement like that with something more than a nod of the head.

By the time he released her mouth, a blush had

restored the color to her cheeks. "Danny! Behave yourself."

"Is that any way to talk to your masterful groom-to-be?"

She elbowed him in the ribs, and he felt better that he had revitalized her good humor—for the moment, at least.

Standing at a counter decorated with hand-drawn hearts laced with the initials of lovers who had preceded them in matrimonial preliminaries, they filled out the forms. Age, date of birth, no prior marriages, no impediments to their coming vows. Except Danny knew Stephanie had never expected to be marrying him and wouldn't be doing it now if it weren't for Edgar's threat.

When they finished, they handed the clerk their completed forms.

She eyed Stephanie's advanced pregnancy and smiled. "I always say, better late than never."

"Yes, ma'am," Danny answered. "I've been meaning to propose for some time. Guess I almost procrastinated too long."

"From the look of your bride, she may not make it to the wedding before that baby of yours pops out."

Frowning and rubbing her hand across her lower back, Stephanie said, "I'll make it even if I have to keep my legs crossed for the full three days."

Danny didn't like the sound of her answer. She wasn't due for another week or more. There should be plenty of time to get the wedding out of the way before Vickie arrived on the scene.

He tucked the signed and stamped marriage license safely in his hip pocket as they walked back to the truck.

"So what do you want to do about the wedding itself?" he asked as casually as he could. The reality of what they'd done—of what they were about to do—was about as scary as being the nozzle man on your first fire.

This time he wouldn't be able to back out, to change his mind, to simply walk away as he had twice before. *As his father had.*

Damn! For Stephanie's sake, Danny wished he could get an instant gene transplant so he wouldn't risk hurting her.

"Under the circumstances," she said, "I'd like to keep it as low-key as we can."

"Yeah. Guess it would be tough to get a wedding gown fitted in only a couple of days."

"Particularly in the shape I'm in. There can't be many places to buy a ready-made maternity wedding gown."

He stopped her on the sidewalk and lifted her chin. "You deserve better, Twigs. A gown and a church, music and dancing. If you want me to—"

With her fingertip on his lips, she silenced him. "This is all so surreal. And it isn't fair to you, either."

"You don't hear me complaining, do you?"

"No, and I suppose you're going to tell me this is what friends are for."

Catching her finger in his mouth, he nibbled lightly.

It nearly broke his heart to see the troubled look in her hazel eyes, the golden sparkles dimmed by worry. Marriage to a guy like him did that to a woman, he supposed, somebody she knew couldn't handle commitment. "I'm gathering lots of points so you'll owe me big time later."

"It figures."

She visibly shuddered, from the cool afternoon air or something else, he couldn't be sure, and he turned them back toward the parking lot.

"I'll talk to my dad this evening about what we're doing."

"You want me to be there with you?"

"I think it will be easier to explain without you."

Probably because Chief Gray hadn't planned for his daughter to marry an ordinary firefighter. Not that Danny couldn't study, take the tests and move up a grade or two. In fact, for Stephanie he'd do just that if she'd ask him to. God, if it were in his power, he'd give her the moon and stars. But he didn't think he'd have the chance, as much as he might want to. The likelihood of their marriage lasting through even one civil service testing cycle seemed remote. Her troubles with Edgar would be resolved by then. She wouldn't need Danny any longer.

"If your dad wants to hit me or something, I'll come on over."

She stopped at the passenger side of the truck and looked up at him. "I suspect Dad will want to give you a medal. He isn't fond of Edgar and he's always had a soft spot for you—even when you hit that home run right through our front window.''

''Really?'' Pleased with that news, he opened the door, helped her up, and caught her when she lost her balance, teetering backwards. ''Easy, Twigs.''

''Thanks.'' Righting herself, she took a deep breath. ''Dad has a friend who's a judge. Maybe he can ask him to perform the ceremony in his chambers. I'd at least like my father there wherever we do the deed.''

''Fine by me.'' Taking her hand, he brushed a kiss to her knuckles. He'd buy her flowers, the biggest bouquet he could find. She deserved so much more. ''Everything's going to work out, Stephanie. You'll see.''

STEPHANIE HELD THAT THOUGHT close to her heart all night. She'd explained the situation to her father, who had taken the news that she was going to marry Danny amazingly well.

The next morning, he went off to a community public relations affair in a bright frame of mind while she'd been blurry eyed from lack of sleep. What was it with the men in her life? Didn't they realize she wanted love, not a forced marriage to protect her child *or* a marriage of convenience?

She stormed around the house. Guilt about what she was doing to Danny was driving her crazy. So was the ache in her back. And every time she heard a car outside, she was half terrified Edgar was about to show up and drag her off where he could snatch her baby right out of her belly. Which didn't seem like all that bad an idea at the moment because little Vickie was pressing on her pelvis as if she was doing a headstand, which was giving Stephanie cramps.

She had to do something to get her mind off her troubles.

The toilet needed cleaning. If there was any job in the world she hated more, Stephanie couldn't think of it. But she might as well get it done while she was feeling energetic. No doubt after the baby arrived, she wouldn't have time for such mundane chores.

She also needed to work on the layout for the Boutique Bagels' ads. She wanted to be able to put draft copies in the mail to the owner before the baby came, let him have time to study the concept, then put the wheels in motion to run the ads when she was back from the hospital. The timing would work out perfectly.

Of course, as long as she was cleaning the toilets she might as well scrub the bathroom floor, too. The kitchen could use a good mopping while she was at it.

And she hadn't packed her bag yet for the hospital. Now, there was something she couldn't put off much longer. She'd get down her suitcase from the attic and find the packing list Maureen had given the class.

Not that there was any rush. She'd seen her doctor on Monday. Everything was progressing normally. She had a full week to go.

DANNY WAS AT LOOSE ENDS.

He had the day off but he didn't want to do any training, not twenty-four hours before the triathlon. He needed his muscles to be relaxed and well rested, ready to perform at top speed. For the sake of the buddies he'd lost in Idaho, he wanted to be at his peak.

Because of Moose, he had to be if he wanted a chance to win.

But with nothing to do his nerves were stretched as tautly as a fire hose under maximum water power. *Tomorrow would be his wedding day.* He could barely believe it even when he said the words aloud. *Twigs, his bride.* He didn't know whether to shout it from the rooftop or send her a sympathy card.

He wanted to race across the street, take her in his arms, kiss her senseless, and tell her that he'd love her forever. Because that was the truth. That astounding discovery had hit him upside the head at about four in the morning, and he hadn't been able to go back to sleep afterwards.

He actually loved *her.* He wasn't going to wake up tomorrow or the next day or ten thousand days from now bored with the whole thing, wanting out of his marriage to Stephanie. Not a chance.

This time he was going to stick it out through sickness and health, until death did them part—unless she told him to get lost.

But the thought of actually crossing the street to announce that revelation was about as absurd as running a marathon on his hands. She wouldn't want to hear it.

In fact, given her nerves yesterday, she was probably on the verge of backing out of the marriage altogether. He wasn't about to risk that.

So he decided to go down to the station house. He could hang out with the guys on B shift, maybe have lunch at the Smoke Eaters Bar and Grill. Stay loose that way. Then he'd carbo-load for the race, get a good night's sleep and be all set to go in the morning.

Yep, that's what he'd do.

TO HIS DISAPPOINTMENT, all the fire trucks were out on a run when he arrived at Station 6. He wandered inside, his running shoes squeaking on the concrete floor of the empty bay. Even the administrative offices sat absent of their usual occupants, Saturday being a day off for the eight-to-fivers.

Out of desperation, he shoved open the door to the dispatch office. There was always someone on duty there.

He almost groaned aloud when he saw Emma Jean behind the counter. Bad mistake, he realized. He didn't want to get trapped into a conversation with her but he couldn't think of a graceful way to escape.

"Hey, hon! I knew you'd drop by today," she said, her silver jewelry jingling as she turned toward him.

"How would you know that?"

Lifting her shoulders in an easy shrug, she grinned. "I'm psychic."

"Yeah, right."

"Anyway, I was checking out my new crystal ball this morning and I saw the darnedest thing." Getting up, she came over to the counter that separated them. "It didn't make any sense to me but maybe you can explain it. Take a look."

The scowl he'd developed since he walked into dispatch deepened. "If you've got another hamster in that damn crystal ball of yours, I'm going to break it open with a fire ax and scatter it at sea."

"Goodness, but you're in a bad mood. I can't think why, not if what I see in this is true." She placed her ball on the counter and pulled the cover away. "What do you think?"

He thought he was crazy. What he saw inside the globe was an image of him holding a baby in his arms, a woman next to him who resembled Stephanie. The picture was fuzzy like an out-of-focus camera shot but the likeness was uncannily accurate.

Sweat beaded his forehead. "How'd you do that?" It was his own imagination that had conjured that picture. Not Emma Jean and her stupid ball.

Emma Jean pumped a fist in the air. "I knew this ball was better than the last one I had! Paid twice as much for it, too, but it was worth every penny."

He took a step away from the counter. "I gotta go." Whirling, he made for the door. He didn't know what was going on.

The last words he heard before making a dash down the hallway were, "Congratulations! She's a lucky woman."

That was so eerie it gave him the creeps. He'd never expected to see *anything* in a crystal ball, except the paper rodent image Emma Jean had planted there. He wasn't psychic. Didn't want to be.

Still, he couldn't shake the thought that he'd had a glimpse of the future, a future he desperately wanted to be more than a fleeting moment in time. His imagination had done that for him.

And the overwhelming love he had for Stephanie.

AFTER A QUICK TRIP DOWNTOWN to do some shopping, he killed most of the afternoon at the Smoke Eaters Bar and Grill, sipping a single beer and playing darts with anyone who showed up.

Finally he went home. The phone was ringing when he walked in the door, a light blinking on the answering machine.

"Sullivan."

"Thank God you're home, Danny. This is Harlan Gray. I think Stephanie has gone into labor but she won't go to the hospital. You'd better get over here in a hurry."

For a full heartbeat, panic immobilized him. Then he broke into a sprint fast enough to break world records in the hundred-yard dash.

Chapter Fourteen

Danny burst in through the back door, nearly scaring Stephanie out of her wits. He looked wild eyed, his face a white mask.

"How far apart are the pains?"

"A long way. They're not even regular. I'm sure they're those practice contractions, those Braxton Hicks thingies." She wouldn't let them be anything else. She wasn't ready to go to the hospital, couldn't have the baby yet. It was too soon. She'd been having aches and pains for weeks, it seemed. These were no different.

"I've been watching her," her father said, looking as anxious as Danny. *Men.* "I think they're about fifteen minutes apart."

She got up to pace around the kitchen. The floor was immaculate, the counters sparkling, every dish put away. "They'll stop in a minute. They already have. See?" She held her arms wide and put on a bright, albeit phony, smile.

"Maybe we ought to call the doctor," Danny suggested.

"Don't be silly. It's the weekend. She needs her time off like everyone else."

"We could go to the hospital, let somebody check you out."

"I'm not even packed yet." She'd been so busy cleaning and scrubbing, she hadn't gotten around to it.

"You're not? God, Stephanie, you were supposed to do that weeks ago."

"Well, I didn't!" she snapped. "The list is around here somewhere. And don't swear at me."

"Right. I'm sorry." He looked suitably contrite—and worried sick.

"I'll get the suitcase down," Harlan said.

"There's no rush," she repeated, more for herself than her father, who was already heading for the pull-down stairs to the attic.

"You want to sit down? Or have me rub your back?"

"No, I want you to go home. Dad will call you if—"

"I'm not leaving."

Stubborn man. "You have to. You've got your race in the morning." And a wedding in the afternoon you'd never intended. "You need your rest."

"Forget the damn—darn—race." Pulling out a chair at the table, he sat down, leaned back and crossed his arms. "I'm going to stay right here until you decide it's time for me to take you to the hospital."

"Danny, the race. What about your friends in Idaho? You were doing it for—"

"You and Vickie are more important than they are."

Unable to stand on her feet any longer, she sat down opposite him. A contraction snaked through her, and she wrapped her arms around her belly, trying not to let the pain show on her face. "You can't let your team down."

"How many minutes since the last one?"

She hadn't fooled him. "I don't know."

Skeptically he raised his eyebrows.

"I don't, really. Dad's been keeping track." She'd been doing her damnedest to ignore the whole thing. With each passing hour, she'd been increasingly afraid this was the real deal, not a false contraction in the bunch. For all her brave words, abject terror kept nipping at her heels. She couldn't talk fast enough, rationalize wildly enough, to keep the fear at bay. "You know as well as I do that I can't have the baby yet."

"I've got the feeling you'll have the baby whenever Vickie decides it's time."

She groaned but not from pain. "I'll mess up everything. Your race—"

"I'll race next year."

"The wedding. There's not much point in getting married if I have the baby before the ceremony."

A frown lowered his brows. "We'll get the judge over here now."

"We have to wait the three days, so no matter what

else I do, I'm going to have to keep my legs crossed until after midnight.''

Her father reappeared in the kitchen with her suitcase. ''Here we go. Now, you say there's a list—''

''I'll take care of it.'' She hopped up too quickly and was rewarded with sharp pain across her groin for her effort. ''Dammit,'' she muttered.

Both Danny and her father eyed her with mild censure.

She planted her fist on her hip. ''It's all right for a woman in labor to swear, and you can expect a hell of a lot more of that from me before this whole mess is over.''

''Ah, so you admit you're in labor,'' Danny said with a self-righteous gleam in his eyes.

Her father set the suitcase down on the floor. ''There's going to be a problem getting Judge Helmet here before tomorrow afternoon. He left after lunch yesterday to go golfing at Pebble Beach and planned to come back tomorrow in time to perform the ceremony. I don't know how to reach him.''

It was Danny's turn to swear under his breath.

''See? I can't have the baby yet.'' Snatching up the suitcase, she marched down the hallway toward her bedroom.

Danny shot to his feet as she left the kitchen. Talk about the best-laid plans going wrong. He wanted this wedding in the worst way, but it wasn't going to happen unless Stephanie thought it was the only way to keep her baby. And he knew darn well no amount of crossing her legs would slow down the arrival of a baby determined to be born. Not at this stage.

"I'll help her get packed, Chief, if you'll give Tommy Tonka a call. Tell him he'll have to move up to the senior division of the triathlon."

"Can he do that?"

"It's within the rules, since he's already registered. But finishing the race…" He shrugged, wishing he hadn't been so set on Paseo winning the event and him personally beating Moose. "Whatever he can do will be better than conceding and withdrawing the whole team." At least Moose and his cohorts from the La Verde Fire Department wouldn't have a total walkover.

"All right, I'll get hold of Tommy. You take care of Stephanie for me."

"I will, assuming she'll let me."

Nodding grimly, Chief Gray acknowledged that would be a major hurdle. "I'll call the Highway Patrol, see if they can locate the judge."

"Thanks." He hesitated. "Chief, I know you probably wouldn't have picked me to marry your daughter, but I want you to know—"

"What makes you think I wouldn't want you to marry Stephanie?"

"Well, I—" His shoulders slumped and he studied the squares of linoleum on the floor. "You know how my dad took off, leaving Mom and me, and it makes sense you'd think I'd do the same thing to Stephanie. But I swear—"

Harlan firmly clamped his hand down on Danny's

shoulder. "Son, I knew your father and while he wasn't a bad man, he was weak. He didn't have the guts to stick around when things got a little rough so he took off. That's not what a man ought to do."

"I know."

"Fortunately, as I watched you grow up, I saw you were a lot like your mother, not your dad."

Danny lifted his head. "I am?"

"There's never been any quit in you, son. You'd literally go through a wall of fire to protect someone you loved. I can't think of anyone I'd rather trust with my daughter's happiness." He slipped his hand around the back Danny's neck and squeezed lightly. "If I'd had a son I would have wanted him to be just like you."

Tears blurred Danny's vision. He'd never realized how much he'd counted on Chief Gray's support, his encouragement, through all those years when he'd been without a father of his own. But he'd never needed to hear his words of encouragement so strongly as he did at this particular moment.

"I'll take care of her, sir. I swear it."

Harlan raised his brows. "Even when she's giving you a hard time?"

Danny's lips twitched into a grin. "Sir, that's when I love her the most."

Swiping the back of his hand across his eyes, Harlan gestured toward Stephanie's bedroom. "She's not going to be easy to live with but you might as well start getting used to it now."

"Yes, sir." Their eyes met in silent communication, then Danny turned away, turned toward the woman who would his wife.

Forever.

He found her standing in the middle of her bedroom, a diaphanous blue-silk nightgown tossed carelessly into her open suitcase on the bed.

And she was crying.

Dammit, she never cried. That she was doing it now nearly broke his heart.

"Hey, Twigs, don't fall apart on me." He took her in his arms and held her.

Trembling, she sniffed at her tears. "It already hurts. How am I going to manage twenty hours more?"

"We're going to do it together. For however long it takes, and you'll be great. You're the strongest, the most determined woman I know when you set your mind to something."

She shivered again. "I'm so scared, Danny."

So was he, but he couldn't admit it. Not to Stephanie. Not when she needed him to be strong for her and their baby.

Their baby. The thought, when it fully formed, nearly drove him to his knees. Vickie was *his* little girl, as well as Stephanie's. Dear God! He was about to be a father. Oh, man, he didn't want to mess this up.

"Let's sit down." His stomach rolled with a combination of terror and excitement as he eased them both down to the edge of the bed. Rubbing her back with one hand, he rested the other on her belly that was tight and hard.

"We're going to take this slow and easy. Real calm." He silently vowed he'd stay calm despite the hysteria that threatened to steal the oxygen from not only his lungs but from the entire room, like a flashover, an explosion of fire and flame. "Now, where's that list we're supposed to follow?"

She gestured toward her dresser. "I forgot to get a tennis ball."

He frowned and blinked. "Tennis? Now?"

"For massaging my lower back. That's where it hurts the most."

"Okay." He remembered now, something about doing a firm countermassage with a ball at the small of her back. "I've got a whole case full of balls at home. We'll get a bunch. What else do we need?"

"I don't know. I can't even think."

"Not to worry, sweetheart." He kissed her temple, the fine hairs there damp with perspiration. He could almost smell her fear, could certainly see it in her eyes. "Remember how Maureen told us to relax? It's early yet."

She grimaced. "Easy for you to say."

"That's my girl, always a smart mouth." He grinned at her, then slipped away. His legs were still as weak as water but he managed to get the list and start checking off the items she was supposed to pack. Lotions and powders, a paper bag in case she hyperventilated—or *he* did—a brush and her pots of makeup from the bathroom. Heavy socks in case her feet got cold. A robe and slippers to go with the nightgown.

Her feminine scents surrounded him, slipped under his skin. Only hours from now she'd be his wife. To have and to hold forever, if she'd let him.

"You certainly know your way around a woman's bedroom," she commented when he dropped a couple of pair of silken undies in the suitcase.

"I read widely."

She choked on a laugh, and that was good. She was beginning to relax, go with the flow.

"Are you keeping track of the time between contractions?" he asked.

"Not really. But they don't seem so bad now."

"See? You're doing great. You should have known I'd never lie to you."

"You've always lied to me. When I was fourteen, you told me I couldn't go to the movies with you because it was a guys-only show. I found out later you took a date."

He frowned. "I don't remember that."

"And when I was nine, you said there wasn't a Santa Claus."

"There isn't," he protested.

"He brought me a ten-speed bicycle that year and a boom box that could blast out the entire neighborhood. No way was I going to stop believing in him."

Laughing, he snapped the suitcase closed. "Okay, you got me. I lied."

Taking his hand, she brought his knuckles to her cheek, rubbing gently. "Thanks. For everything."

A knot formed in his throat so big he didn't think he could talk. He'd give her Santa Claus and the Easter Bunny, too, if that's what she wanted. And the Tooth Fairy for Vickie when the time came.

She squeezed his hand more tightly, and he knew she was having another contraction. They might have slowed but they were real. They had to be. She was in too much pain for her to be in false labor.

"You want to call the doctor yet?" he asked.

"No, but I could use a back rub if you don't have anything better to do."

"You got it, sweetheart."

Lying down on the bed, she curled onto her side and he began massaging the small of her back like they'd practiced in class. Except this was different. This was the real deal.

Her father poked his head in the door. "Everything okay?"

"We're fine, thanks," Danny said.

"Anything I can do, you let me know."

"Don't worry, Dad." She gave him a brave smile. "Women have been doing this for years."

"I wish your mother were here. She'd know what to do."

"She'd probably hover and drive me crazy like you're doing."

He laughed. "I'll go boil some water or something. Call me if you need me."

Danny kept rubbing her back, easing the tension between her shoulder blades, helping her through the relaxation exercises they'd learned. When the contractions remained about fifteen minutes apart, they got out a pinochle game as a distraction. Stephanie double skunked him.

Stretching, she eased off the bed and stood. ''I think I'll go—'' Her eyes widened and she stood perfectly still. ''Oh, my God!''

''What? What's wrong?'' Fear punched through him, so strong it was like a fire ax embedded in his chest.

''My water. I think it broke.''

An instant later, she groaned and reached for his arm, her fingers digging into his flesh, and he knew it was time to get her to the hospital.

SOME VICIOUS CREATURE had gotten inside her and was ripping her apart, clawing and stretching, pushing and pulling.

''Remember to breathe, Twigs. Let's count it together. Six, seven, eight…''

She looked up into Danny's beautiful blue eyes, the eyes she loved so well, and *hated* him. ''Oh, God…''

''You're almost there, sweetheart. You're doing great. It's peaking now. Almost over. Slide down the other side and relax.''

''Relax?'' She puffed out a breath as the contraction finally eased. ''Are you out of your mind? It hurts like hell!''

''Yeah, I know.''

''You can't possibly know!''

He wiped her forehead with a damp cloth and slipped a piece of ice between her lips. She was so glad Danny was with her, she could have wept, but she no longer had the energy.

"What time is it?" she asked.

He glanced at his watch. "Eleven-thirty."

"Any sign of the judge?"

"No. I'm going to send for the hospital chaplain."

"Oh, he'll be thrilled to come out in the middle of the night to perform a wedding ceremony. Maybe we can get an organist to drop by, too."

"I figure by the time we're finished, every nurse in the hospital will be crying."

"Why? Because you'll be out of circulation?"

"Naw. Women always cry at weddings."

She grabbed his hand, threading her fingers through his. "Danny, maybe we ought to forget about the marriage. There's only an outside chance anyway that we can beat Edgar and all his attorneys."

"We'll beat him, sweetheart. There's no way in hell I'm going to let him steal our baby away from us."

"*Our* baby?"

His expression softened. "Yours and mine. I've already got a plan to build her a dollhouse in the backyard, and I'm going to teach her to ride a bike and fly a kite and swing on a swing. All that good kind of stuff, you know?"

"Oh, Danny." Tears flooded her eyes. "How can you say that when she's not even—"

He hushed Stephanie with a kiss. "In every way that counts, Vickie is my daughter. I love her."

What about her? Stephanie wanted to ask, but a

new contraction began building, snaking inside her, gripping her so tightly, she wanted to scream. She held back, breathing as Danny coached her, and felt her heart break because he hadn't said he loved her, too.

As the pain eased, the nurse came bustling into the labor room. "How're we doing, folks?"

"The contractions are coming every three to four minutes and last almost a minute," Danny answered efficiently. "They're getting pretty strong."

"A man of great understatement," Stephanie muttered. Danny's emergency training made him sound so damn calm, she wanted to rip out his eyes.

"Let me take a look."

Stephanie tried to relax while the nurse peered under the sheet, poking and prodding her. Total lack of modesty appeared to be a prerequisite for having a baby.

"You're doing beautifully," the nurse said, all bubbly and upbeat. "You're dilated to seven centimeters. Won't be long now."

"Only seven?" Stephanie groaned. After all this time she should be at *twenty!* Big enough to give birth to an elephant. A full-grown one!

"Could you arrange for the hospital chaplain to come see us?" Danny asked.

The nurse looked up with sympathetic eyes. "Prayer is always good at times like this."

"Actually we'd like to get married. As soon after midnight as we can."

"Married?" Her jaw dropped. "I'm not sure—"

"It's important, ma'am."

Another contraction overtook Stephanie while Danny and the nurse discussed the relative merits of a hasty marriage, unwed mothers and illegitimate children. She gritted her teeth through the pains, and when they eased she raised up on the bed and glared at the nurse. "Get the damn chaplain in here on the double or I'm going to go looking for him myself!"

The nurse's eyes widened. "Yes, of course. I'll see if I can locate him. And your doctor, too."

"See that you do." Stephanie collapsed back onto the bed. "I'm turning into a witch," she said with a sigh.

"A lovely witch, if I do say so myself."

"You're only saying that so I won't cast a spell on you."

"You cast a spell on me a long time ago, Twiggy. I just didn't realize it at the time."

She looked at him blankly. Could he possibly mean—

Another pain rose faster and harder than those that had preceded it, ruthlessly pounding, grinding, making it impossible to think.

"It's happening too fast—" she cried before she was no longer able to speak at all.

"Just don't push yet," Danny pleaded. "The preacher will be here soon."

In a daze, one contraction after another swept over her, leaving her little time to recover. Dr. Pamela Ulrich arrived, looking pleased with her patient's progress. A cheery gentleman with gray hair, bright blue eyes and a minister's collar appeared, taking up a position beside her as the nurses wheeled her into the delivery room. Harlan Gray joined the entourage of witnesses all gowned in green.

"I'm sorry, honey. I know your mother wanted both you and Karen to have big weddings," her father said. "Guess it's not going to work out for either of you."

"It's okay, Dad. I don't think there's enough time to plan all the—" She groaned, trying to choke back a scream.

"Do you want some pain medicine?" Danny asked.

Though she would have liked about a gallon of whatever they had to give her, she shook her head. "I'd like to be able to remember my wedding."

Through her pain she saw a wry smile that didn't quite hide the depth of his concern. "I think this one is going to be truly memorable."

"Mr. Sullivan," the nurse said, "there's a young man in the waiting room, a Tommy Tonka. He's asking to talk with you. He says he hasn't been able to sleep."

"I'm pretty busy."

"Why don't you have him come on in?" Stephanie bit down as the peak of the contraction passed. "He can be your best man."

"Really?"

"Danny, I just want this whole thing over and done with."

Taking another look at her, Dr. Ulrich said, "Reverend, if you're going to get this couple married before the baby puts in an appearance, you'd better hurry it up. She's crowning.''

''Oh, God.'' Stephanie groaned.

''Don't push,'' Danny ordered.

The door to the delivery room opened to admit Tommy with Emma Jean Witkowsky right behind him, dangling silver earrings flashing in the bright lights. ''I had a vision in my crystal ball,'' she explained. ''I hope you don't mind.''

Stephanie forced herself not to scream in either pain or dismay. ''No problem,'' she gasped. ''You're the designated bridesmaid.''

''I'd be honored.''

''Could somebody please lock that door?'' Danny requested.

Vaguely Stephanie was aware of the wedding party gathering around the head of the delivery table while the doctor watched from the critical spot between her knees, ready to catch the baby. But Stephanie only had eyes for Danny, her groom, the wonderfully handsome man who held her hand while she dug her fingernails into his palm. He looked as disheveled as she felt but the smile on his face was downright possessive and thoroughly masculine. Almost as if—

''Do you take this man—'' the minister began, then turned in question to Danny. ''Your name is—''

''Daniel Michael Sullivan,'' Danny provided, still smiling at her.

''To have and to hold—''

''Let's hurry it up, Reverend,'' the doctor said.

"I do," Stephanie managed to say, not interested in the details of the vow she was about to take. The urge to push was incredible, irresistible, but she fought it, panting, focusing on Danny and the love she felt for him. For the sacrifice he was making.

"And I take Stephanie Ann Gray as my wife, to have and to hold, to love and to cherish, in sickness and in health, for so long as we both shall live."

Let his words be true, the conviction in his voice genuine, she prayed as he slipped a golden band onto her finger. When had he had the chance to—

"Now, by the power vested in me by God and the State of California, I pronounce you—"

"Time's up. Let's get our new daddy down here so he can catch his baby girl."

"—man and wife."

Danny kissed her sweet and fast, and she pushed. Hard. And her father stepped into position beside her, holding her, as Danny moved to the foot of the delivery table. She cried out because she couldn't help herself.

"Easy now," the doctor ordered.

Lifting her head, she watched Danny settle next to the doctor. He looked up and their eyes met, his expression so intense, so perfectly focused on her that she felt filled with his strength and purpose.

"Vickie's coming," he whispered.

"Don't drop her." Stephanie pushed, still watching him and the smile that shone in his eyes. She felt the baby move, slide from her body.

"I've got her head. She's beautiful, like you."

Tears poured from Stephanie's eyes as the doctor told her, "One more time."

And then she saw Vickie's head for herself, her hair dark and matted, and her perfect little body held firmly and protectively in her husband's big, gentle hands. In his eyes she saw the same tears of joy and awe that were blurring her vision.

The baby gave out a lusty cry, and in that moment Stephanie knew she'd never experience a greater love than she felt right then, both for her husband and the baby he held.

"I HOPE WE DON'T HAVE TO GO through that again anytime soon." Sitting in a chair next to Stephanie's hospital bed, Danny felt completely exhausted but he had so much adrenaline still swimming through his veins, there was no possibility he'd be able to sleep. It was like coming down after a big fire. Not something you could do in a few minutes, or even an hour or two.

Apparently Stephanie was having the same problem.

"She was worth every moment." Holding Vickie in the crook of her arm, Stephanie smiled at their sleeping baby.

"Seems to me I recall a couple of times when you referred to her as a monster."

"I didn't say any such thing." She blinked at him innocently.

In response, he shook his head and gave his wife a faint smile. "I'll never tell."

Wife. He still couldn't get over the knowledge that they were married. They had a daughter. The three of them were a *family.* Nor had he ever been filled with such astounding love as that moment when Vickie slid into his hands, all slick and wet, and crying almost before she was fully free of Stephanie's womb. And he'd looked up to see his wife crying, too.

He'd already relived that experience a thousand times. With each reliving, his love for both his wife and daughter had grown more potent until it was a force that would never be broken. He vowed that with his life—his very soul.

In the hours since the birth, and after the crowd of witnesses had finally left them alone, he'd brushed Stephanie's hair for her. She'd put on some lipstick and her nightgown. Given her recent ordeal, she looked better than she had any right to.

A tiny frown formed on her forehead. "Did Tommy ever tell you why he showed up at the hospital?"

"He was a nervous wreck about doing the triathlon in the senior division. I told him he only had to give it his best shot. Winning wasn't important."

She glanced out the window by her bed where the sky was beginning to lighten with the new day. "There's still time for you to run in the race."

"Not me. My place is here with you and our baby."

Stephanie swallowed an unexpected sob. On the constant verge of tears from fatigue and an overload of emotion, tears flooded her eyes as they had so many times in the past few hours. "I feel so guilty I've made you give up so much, forcing you into—"

"Whoa! Wait a minute. I'have haven't given up anything."

"You've given up the race. Given up being a bachelor." At least for the moment. "I've tied you down to the pesky girl across the street when you never would have—"

"Ah, Twigs, sweetheart, don't you know what you've given me?" He shifted from the chair to sit on the edge of her bed. Unable to resist, his finger strayed to the baby's incredibly soft cheek and then to Stephanie's. Their gazes held, and he felt his heart soften. He bent to brush a kiss to her lips.

"You've taught me that I'm capable of love. Not just a casual, how-are-you-doing love, not a relationship for a week or two, one I'll get bored with, but something that's going to last forever. A commitment that's for a lifetime."

The thrill of his words sent a river of joy through her, pressing even more tears to her eyes. "You love me?"

He blinked as though surprised by her comment. "Haven't I mentioned that?"

"Not that I recall. But then, I've been pretty distracted lately." And her hormones were so far into overdrive, she wanted to be sure she'd heard him correctly. "Tell me again."

Reversing his position so he was right next to her, he lifted her with one arm and wrapped his other around both her and their baby.

"I love you Stephanie Sullivan, my wife, my bride, and I love our baby girl. I'll love you both as long as the sun keeps coming up in the morning and I have any breath in me. If I have my way, I'll love you for all eternity. You see, you've turned me into a real commitment kind of guy."

Her chin trembled. It was true, what she'd seen in his eyes, what she'd prayed she'd heard from his heart.

"I love you, too, Danny Sullivan. Because you're irreverent and brave, and because you make me laugh. I loved you when I was fourteen years old, and I've never stopped loving you. I never will, not for all of eternity."

"I think I loved you back then, too, which is why I teased you so much. But face it—" He gave her quick wink. "I had to wait until you grew up before I could make my move."

She laughed, then winced at the pain she'd caused herself. "I'm all grown up now."

"Yeah, you are." And with a kiss that was both sweet and tender, filled with promises, he showed her just how much he loved her and always would.

With every ounce of her being, she responded, letting him know she felt exactly the same way.

Epilogue

Three months later

Danny took a slice of white layer cake and slipped a bite into Stephanie's mouth as she fed him a matching piece, still carefully holding Vickie in one arm as she had during the marriage ceremony. A crumb fell onto the baby's frilly pink dress. He plucked it up, feeding her with his fingertips.

The wedding guests, who were circled around them for the cake-cutting, laughed and clapped.

"Danny!" Stephanie admonished him sternly, although the gold sparkles in her hazel eyes danced with happiness. "She's too little for cake."

"Hey, she's an important part of the celebration. I don't want her to miss out on anything."

"I doubt, with you as her daddy, there'll be a thing in the world she'll have to do without."

Danny's heart filled with gratitude that he wouldn't have to go to court to fight to keep Vickie as his daughter. Apparently Edgar's mother had lost interest when she heard her son had sired a daughter rather than a male child to whom he could pass on his name. That was just fine with Danny. He could already tell from her cute little smile that she was going to be a Sullivan through and through.

Within the first few days after Vickie's birth, Stephanie's father had begun to insist that he wanted a formal wedding for his daughter. Though nervous about standing up in front of all his friends, Danny thought it was a good idea, too. His bride deserved the very best.

Councilwoman Anderson had volunteered her beautifully landscaped backyard for the event; Judge Helmet, who had arrived tardy for the first marriage ceremony, had performed the second with grand pomp and circumstance, his black robe fluttering in the warm summer breeze.

Waiting for Stephanie beneath a rose trellis in full bloom, Danny's heart had nearly seized when he saw her walking down the aisle dressed all in white, Vickie in her arms instead of a bouquet of flowers. Nothing could have been more perfect.

Greg Wells served as his best man this time around, then took up his guitar to play a soft rendition of Elton John's "Can You Feel the Love Tonight?" There wasn't a dry eye in the place.

Danny's mom had been in the front row with her new husband. Stephanie's sister Karen and her children were part of the wedding party, although her husband was out of the country on deployment with the Marines.

All in all, a perfect wedding day, although no more memorable than their first, Danny decided with a grin. He'd make sure this wedding night was one to remember, too.

As the crowd began to disperse, Tommy came up to him to say goodbye, a cute little redhead on his arm and a bronze third-place team triathlon medal on a ribbon around his neck.

"Thanks for inviting us," Tommy said, a blush creeping up his neck.

"You're welcome, kid." He extended his hand to the young man. "The Paseo Fire Department owes you big time. You're one of us now."

"I wish we could have taken first."

"It doesn't matter. You beat La Verde, and that's what counts." Fortunately Moose had pulled up lame halfway through the race, not finishing at all. Not that Danny would wish his nemesis an injury, of course.

"I watched Tommy race," Rachel said shyly. "He was wonderful."

The youngster's blush flamed as bright as a brush-fire in a high wind.

Chuckling to himself, Danny turned to find Stephanie and Emma Jean huddled together in deep conversation and giggling.

"All right, ladies. Sounds to me like you two are up to no good."

"Oh, it's definitely good," Stephanie insisted. "Emma Jean's been reading her Tarot cards."

"Oh, no," Danny groaned. "You don't believe that stuff, do you?"

Emma Jean tossed her head dramatically, making her earrings shimmer. "You know perfectly well that I have psychic powers."

"Yeah, right." He didn't know how she'd managed to show up at the hospital in time for the wedding—or what he'd seen in her crystal ball—but he wasn't going to credit any paranormal nonsense.

Stephanie tucked her free arm through his. "If she's right this time, it's Greg Wells who'll be the next to hear wedding bells."

Danny barked a laugh. "Greg? No way. That cowboy has no intention of getting himself roped into matrimony."

Smiling smugly, Stephanie said, "Neither did you, hotshot. Neither did you."

A royal monarch's search for an heir leads
him to three American princesses in

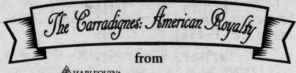

The Carradignes: American Royalty

from

◆ HARLEQUIN®

AMERICAN *Romance*®

King Easton's second choice for the crown is
Princess Amelia Carradigne, the peacekeeper of
the family. But Amelia has a little secret of her own...her
clandestine marriage to a mercenary—
under an assumed name. Now news of her unlawful union
has been leaked to the press and her
"husband" has returned for some answers!

Don't miss:

THE UNLAWFULLY WEDDED PRINCESS
by Kara Lennox   April 2002

And check out these other titles in the series:

THE IMPROPERLY PREGNANT PRINCESS
by Jacqueline Diamond   March 2002

THE SIMPLY SCANDALOUS PRINCESS
by Michele Dunaway   May 2002

And a tie-in title from
HARLEQUIN®
INTRIGUE®

THE DUKE'S COVERT MISSION
by Julie Miller   June 2002

Available at your favorite retail outlet.

HARLEQUIN®
Makes any time special®

Meet the Randall brothers...four sexy bachelor brothers who are about to find four beautiful brides!

WYOMING WINTER

by bestselling author

Judy Christenberry

In preparation for the long, cold Wyoming winter, the eldest Randall brother seeks to find wives for his four single rancher brothers...and the resulting matchmaking is full of surprises! Containing the first two full-length novels in Judy's famous *4 Brides for 4 Brothers* miniseries, this collection will bring you into the lives, and loves, of the delightfully engaging Randall family.

Look for WYOMING WINTER in March 2002.

And in May 2002 look for SUMMER SKIES, containing the last two Randall stories.

HARLEQUIN®
Makes any time special®

Coming in April 2002
from

HARLEQUIN®

AMERICAN *Romance*®

and

Judy
Christenberry

RANDALL RICHES
(HAR #918)

Desperate to return to his Wyoming ranch, champion bull
rider Rich Randall had no choice but to accept sassy
Samantha Jeffer's helping hand—with a strict
"no hanky-panky" warning. But on the long road home
something changed and Rich was suddenly thinking of
turning in his infamous playboy status
for a little band of gold.

Don't miss this heartwarming addition to the series,

Brides
for Brothers

Available wherever Harlequin books are sold.

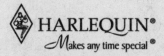
HARLEQUIN®
Makes any time special ®

Visit us at www.eHarlequin.com

HARRR